Read to Me Grandma

3-Minute Stories

publications international, ltd.

Louis Weber, C.E.O.
Publications International, Ltd.
7373 North Cicero Avenue
Lincolnwood, Illinois 60712

www.pubint.com

ISBN: 0-7853-7579-1

CONTENTS

CONTENTS

CONTENTS

Read to Me, Grandma

Written by Joanna Spathis
Illustrated by Denise Hilton Campbell,
Joyce Shelton, and Jody Wheeler

When you ask me to read to you,
with your gentle voice so sweet,
I look into your bright, wide eyes
and quickly take a seat.
For in this world, I promise,
there is nothing I'd rather do
than sit and share this storybook
with a child as dear as you.

On every page inside this book
I know we're sure to find
stories to make our hearts soar
and adventures of every kind.
There are tales of friendship,
of courage, and of might.
There are tales of family,
of love, and even flight!

CONTENTS

Read to Me, Grandma

Written by Joanna Spathis
Illustrated by Denise Hilton Campbell,
Joyce Shelton, and Jody Wheeler

When you ask me to read to you,
with your gentle voice so sweet,
I look into your bright, wide eyes
and quickly take a seat.
For in this world, I promise,
there is nothing I'd rather do
than sit and share this storybook
with a child as dear as you.

On every page inside this book
I know we're sure to find
stories to make our hearts soar
and adventures of every kind.
There are tales of friendship,
of courage, and of might.
There are tales of family,
of love, and even flight!

Someone shared these tales with me
when I was small like you,
and now I trust that they will be
in your life forever, too!
Of course I'll read to you, my dear,
it fills my heart with pride
that I could be the lucky one
to read right by your side.

The Ugly Duckling

Adapted by John O'Grady
Illustrated by Mike Jaroszko

High upon her unhatched egg, the mother duck sat for yet another night. Her duckling was taking its time. The sixth egg was larger than the others. It was a different color, too.

The mother duck spoke to it. "Come now, little one. All of your brothers and sisters are waiting for you!"

With those words, a crack began to grow in the shell of the sixth egg. Then the egg rocked gently.

The mother duck smiled as her last duckling broke through its shell. "Aren't you a large duckling!" she quacked.

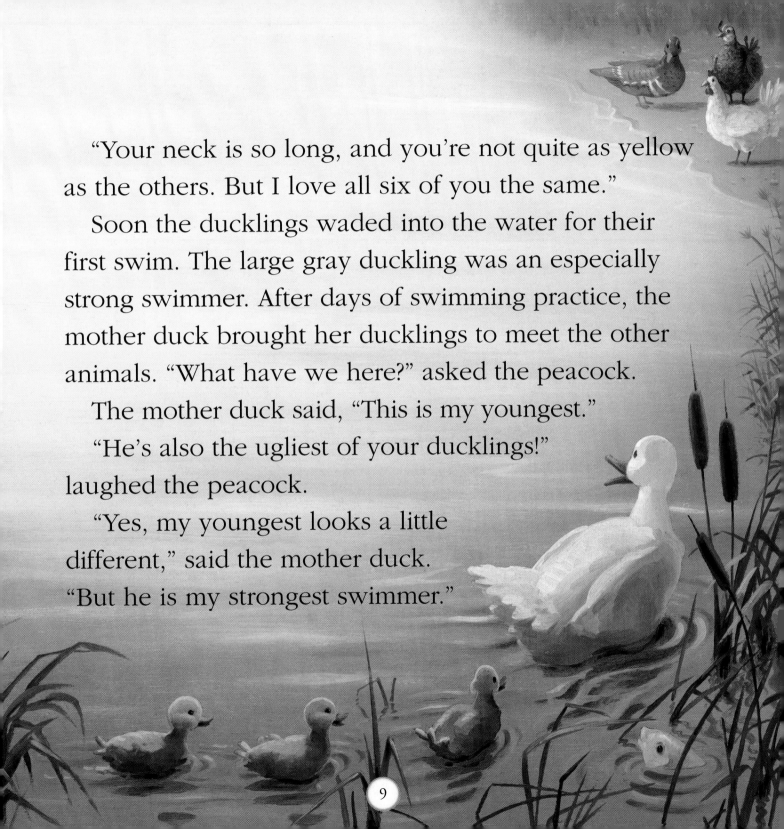

"Your neck is so long, and you're not quite as yellow as the others. But I love all six of you the same."

Soon the ducklings waded into the water for their first swim. The large gray duckling was an especially strong swimmer. After days of swimming practice, the mother duck brought her ducklings to meet the other animals. "What have we here?" asked the peacock.

The mother duck said, "This is my youngest."

"He's also the ugliest of your ducklings!" laughed the peacock.

"Yes, my youngest looks a little different," said the mother duck. "But he is my strongest swimmer."

9

The mother duck gathered her ducklings. "Pay no mind to the peacock," she told them. "Remember, I love all of you the same."

But the ugly duckling felt terrible. That night he decided he must run away and let the rest of his family enjoy the pond without him. When he was sure that everyone was fast asleep, the ugly duckling walked into the night. When the sun rose the next day, the ugly duckling found himself at the edge of a new pond. Geese lived on this pond. "Are you lost, duckling?" one goose asked.

"No, I am not lost," said the ugly duckling. "I have run away from home."

The Ugly Duckling

"We were just going to fly away ourselves," said the goose. "You are welcome to fly with us."

The ugly duckling felt very lucky to have met such friends. But just as the ugly duckling started to say he would fly with them, a big, howling dog leaped from the grasses and startled the flock of geese. The geese flew into the air and quickly out of sight.

The ugly duckling hid among the cattails. Afraid to move, he sat there for hours. Day turned into night, and the dog did not return. But neither did the geese.

The geese knew something that the ugly duckling did not. Winter was coming, and they needed to travel to warmer waters. This would be the duckling's first winter.

With winter came wind, ice, and bitter cold. The ugly duckling was also very lonely. More and more, he missed his mother. He also missed his brothers, sisters, and the warm waters of their pond.

One night the ugly duckling had a wonderful dream. A fire warmed his feathers, and walls held off the wind and snow. Not wishing to wake up, the ugly duckling opened just one eye. A cat and a hen were peering at him!

"Where am I?" asked the ugly duckling.

"Our old woman found you," said the cat.

"She brought you home so you could thaw out."

Each day, the ugly duckling sat by the window and watched for signs of spring. Soon he decided it was time to leave. For days the ugly duckling walked and walked, searching for a place where he could rest and stay warm.

Finally he came to a marsh, where he curled up inside a hollow tree. The snow soon melted, the marsh came alive, and birds returned to their nests.

One morning the duckling awoke to find four swans gliding on the water. "Good morning, swans," said the ugly duckling.

"I am sorry to make you look at me," continued the ugly duckling, "but I must swim to find food."

"You are a pleasure to see!" said one of the swans.

"Your feathers are like pure snow, and your neck is so long and graceful," said another swan.

"Please do not mock me," said the ugly duckling.

The largest swan swam to his side. "Open your eyes, friend," said the swan. "We do not mock you."

The ugly duckling glanced at his reflection in the water. It was the most beautiful swan he had ever seen. "That is me?" he asked the large swan.

"Of course that is you," the large swan said gently.

"Where is your family? Why are you alone?"

The beautiful new swan told his tale to the other swans. "And I still miss my mother," he said. "She loved me even when I was an ugly duckling. Now I am afraid I will never see her again."

"We will help you find her," said the large swan.

So the five swans flew off on their search. Soon they reached that special pond where a mother once sat patiently waiting for her eggs to hatch.

"Mother, I'm back home!" said the beautiful swan who was once an ugly duckling. And his mother still loved him just the same, whether he was an ugly duckling or a beautiful swan.

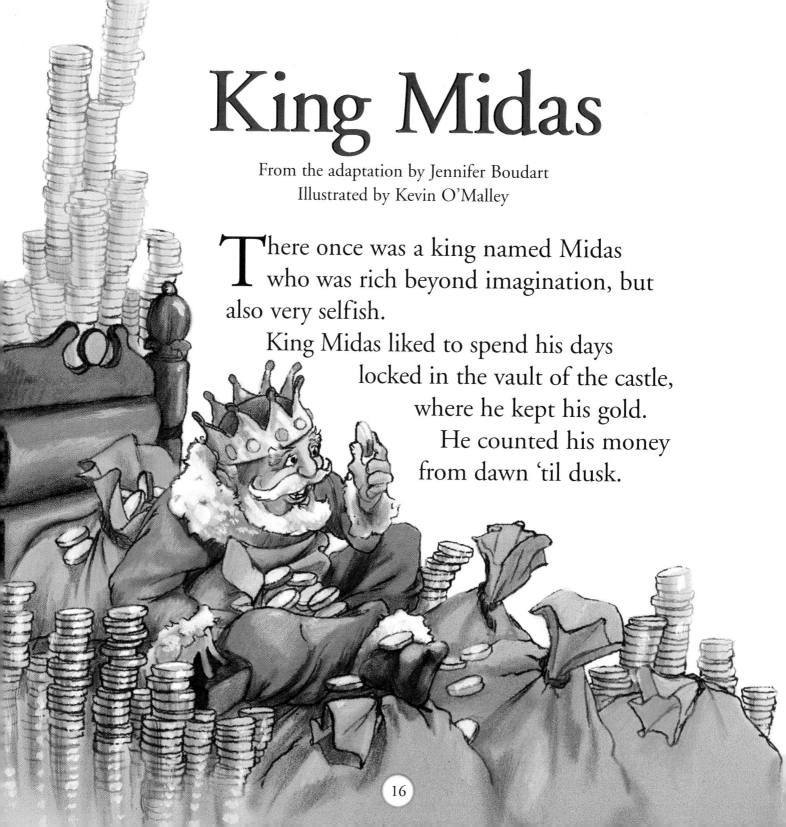

King Midas

From the adaptation by Jennifer Boudart
Illustrated by Kevin O'Malley

There once was a king named Midas who was rich beyond imagination, but also very selfish.

King Midas liked to spend his days locked in the vault of the castle, where he kept his gold. He counted his money from dawn 'til dusk.

King Midas had a daughter named Marygold, who liked to spend her days outdoors among the roses in the garden. There was nothing Marygold liked better than smelling their sweet scent.

One morning, Marygold said, "Father, won't you join me in the garden today?"

"Oh no, Marygold," King Midas replied. "There is so much gold to count. I really must go down to the vault right away."

This saddened Marygold. She was certain that her father would enjoy her roses if he ever saw them in full bloom.

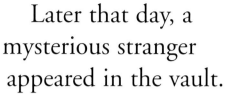

Later that day, a
mysterious stranger
appeared in the vault.
    "Good afternoon,
Your Majesty," said
the stranger.
    "How did you get
in here?" asked King
Midas angrily.
    "Never mind that," said
the stranger. "I have come
to offer you the power to turn
all that you touch into gold."
    "I would like that very much indeed!"
said the greedy Midas.
    "Very well," said the stranger. "After the next
sunrise, anything you touch will turn to gold." With
that, the stranger disappeared.

As promised, King Midas awoke the next morning with a magical touch. He ran from room to room, turning things into solid gold.

King Midas rushed outside to Marygold's garden. He touched a rose and it turned from scarlet red to golden yellow.

"How delighted Marygold will be," Midas said, "when she finds I have turned all her flowers into precious gold."

Soon the king's stomach began to rumble.

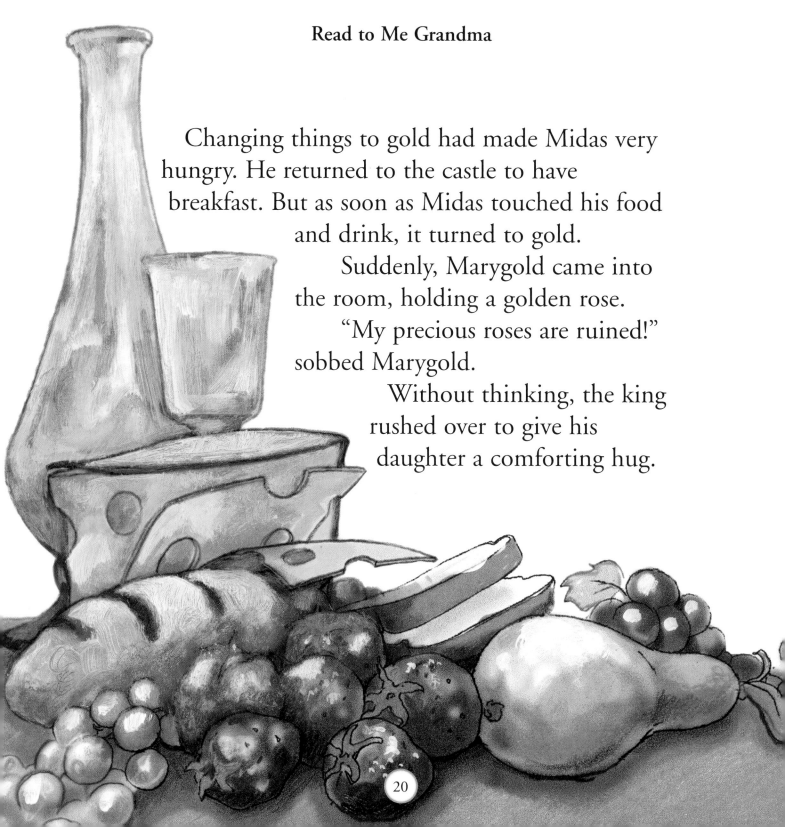

Changing things to gold had made Midas very hungry. He returned to the castle to have breakfast. But as soon as Midas touched his food and drink, it turned to gold.

Suddenly, Marygold came into the room, holding a golden rose.

"My precious roses are ruined!" sobbed Marygold.

Without thinking, the king rushed over to give his daughter a comforting hug.

As soon as King Midas touched her, Marygold turned into solid gold!

King Midas was shocked at what he had done. He now knew that his magic touch was a curse, not a blessing. How could he have been so greedy?

Just then, the mysterious stranger returned and asked, "Aren't you pleased with all your gold, King Midas?"

"I don't care about gold anymore," answered Midas. "I just want Marygold back."

"I see you have learned a lesson," said the stranger. "To get your daughter back, go dive into the river. Bring back enough water to sprinkle over the things you have turned to gold, and they will return to normal."

Midas and his servants ran to the river. Midas leaped into the water. The servants quickly filled their buckets before all the water completely changed to gold.

Back at the castle, King Midas splashed water over Marygold. She instantly turned back into herself.

Together, Midas and Marygold went outside and changed all the golden flowers back into beautiful red roses.

"I promise never to waste any more days counting my gold," King Midas said, giving Marygold another hug.

Finally, King Midas had learned that there are more important things in life than gold.

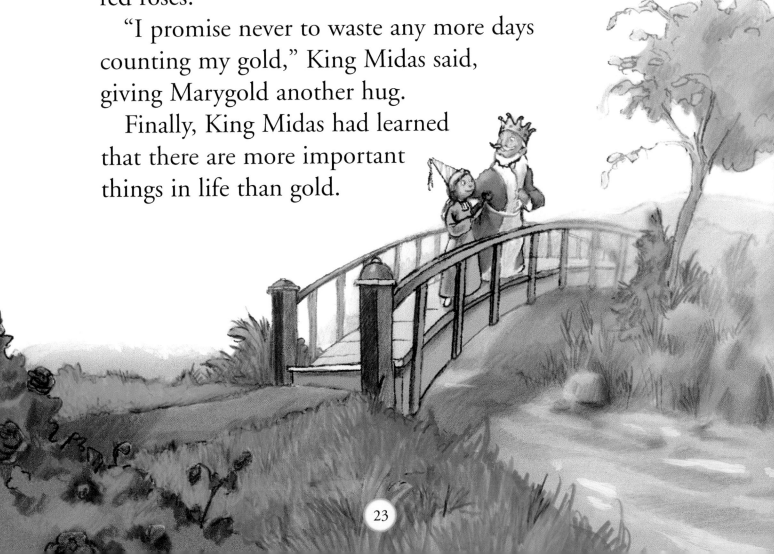

Rip Van Winkle

Adapted by Pegeen Hopkins
Illustrated by John Lund

If the legends of old are true, there is a touch of magic in the Catskill Mountains. Many years ago, a simple, friendly man lived in a town at the base of those mysterious mountains. His name was Rip Van Winkle.

Rip had a wife and several children. He was a kind neighbor, loved by everyone in town. When he walked through the streets, children asked for piggyback rides. Even the neighborhood dogs loved him.

One afternoon, Rip Van Winkle wandered to the top of one of the highest mountains. Suddenly he heard someone call his name. He turned and saw no one.

"Rip Van Winkle," he heard once more. Rip looked around again. This time, his eyes fell on a strange little man climbing toward him.

On his shoulder, the little man carried a huge barrel. "Would you help me with this?" the little man asked.

"Of course," Rip replied. They soon entered a large clearing, where Rip saw a strange group of little men. When Rip and the little man reached the group, one man took the barrel from Rip's hands and poured a dark liquid into a strange cup. The men motioned for Rip to drink it.

Once Rip had finished several cups, he felt tired. His eyes drooped, his vision blurred, and he drifted off into a deep sleep.

When Rip finally opened his eyes, it was morning. Rip was lying right where he had been when he first met the little man.

"Have I been asleep here all night?" Rip exclaimed in a panic. "Mrs. Van Winkle is going to be so angry! What will I tell her?"

Rip started down the mountain feeling a bit confused. As he got to his village, people looked at him with surprise. No one in town looked familiar to Rip. The people did not know Rip, and he did not know them.

Finally, Rip looked down to see what everyone was staring at. A long beard flowed down to his knees!

"Does anybody here know Rip Van Winkle?" Rip asked a group of people.

A tall man asked Rip, "Just exactly who are you?"

"I was myself," Rip said. "I fell asleep on the mountain. Now everything has changed."

Right then a young woman came forward. Rip was sure he had seen her face before, but she had grown up. "What is your father's name?" Rip asked.

"Oh, Rip Van Winkle was his name," said the woman. "It has been twenty years since he took off into the mountains. We have heard nothing about him since."

"And what about your mother?" Rip asked.

"She just recently passed away," said the woman. Hearing this, Rip could no longer contain himself. "I am your father," he cried as he hugged her. "Once I was young Rip Van Winkle. Now I am old Rip Van Winkle. Doesn't anyone know me?"

An old woman walked right up to Rip and put her face almost against his so she could see clearly. "Sure enough," said the old woman. "Welcome home, Rip Van Winkle. Where have you been all these years?"

It did not take Rip long to tell his story. He could not believe he had missed watching his children grow. His wife was dead now. Much of his life had passed in one night. The townspeople listened, amazed. Some people regarded old Rip Van Winkle as the unluckiest man in town. But other people did not believe that a man could sleep for twenty years. Do you?

Little Ant Goes to School

Adapted by Brian Conway
Illustrated by Richard Bernal

Little Andy Ant used to spend each day with his pull toy, happily playing outside in the warm summer sun. Then, as the summer days got shorter, the sun did not feel so warm anymore.

"Summer is over," Andy's mother told him. "That means today is your first day of school!"

Andy had heard about school. He did not want to be cooped up inside all day long.

School was a strange new place. Little Andy Ant was not ready to go. He was scared and a little sad. Then he thought of an idea.

"Can I take my toy along with me?" asked Andy.

"School is for children," his mother answered, "not for toys."

Little Andy Ant tried to be brave. His mother walked him to school that day. "Maybe school won't be so bad once you give it a try," she said. So Andy agreed to try school for just one day.

At school Andy had his very own desk. Teacher gave the children lots of things to do.

Everybody got their own paper and pens. Then they learned all about reading and writing.

Soon Andy started to think about all sorts of new and exciting things.

"Ants work together to make anthills," Andy said to Teacher. "And I think letters work together the same way to make words."

Teacher said Andy was right! He was pretty good at drawing and painting and numbers, too.

Little Andy Ant strolled home from school after a long day. Learning new things was fun!

"Maybe you were right," little Andy Ant told his mother. "Maybe school is not so bad after all."

Andy decided to try school for one more day.

The morning passed by quickly for Andy. Before he knew it, it was already lunchtime. The lunch lady called out, "Cookies and milk!"

What a commotion that caused! Little Andy Ant squeezed his way through and got one tiny chunk of a cookie. Then Andy knew what all the fuss was about. The lunch lady made the best cookies he had ever tasted!

At the end of the day, Andy walked home from school. "Maybe you were right, Mom," said Andy. "Maybe school is not so bad after all."

Andy thought he would try school for another day. As soon as he arrived at school, Teacher told everyone that they were going to the woods on a field trip.

Andy learned about new plants and berries at every turn. Some older children wanted to make a campfire with their teacher, but they needed Andy's help.

"I know how to get the best twigs," Andy said. He whistled for his friend Tweeter Bird.

Tweeter Bird brought back the finest twigs in the woods. There were enough twigs to build a campfire and for each little ant to roast a marshmallow.

Everyone liked Andy and his friend Tweeter very much. Andy had a big smile on his face when he walked home.

Andy not only had his own desk at school, but there were things like field trips and recess, too!

"Maybe you were right, Mom," said little Andy Ant. "Maybe school is not so bad after all."

The next day, Andy wanted to try school again. He did not know what to expect in school that day, but he had an idea it might be fun.

Little Andy Ant walked to school and sat down at his desk. One of the children in his class turned to Andy and said, "I would like you to come to my birthday party today."

After school, Andy raced home. Up until then, he thought birthdays only happened once a year, when he celebrated his own birthday.

Now Andy learned he could celebrate his birthday *and* his friends' birthdays, too!

"I think you were right, Mom," said little Andy Ant. "Maybe school is not so bad after all."

Andy had fun at his school friend's party. He ate some delicious birthday cake and even got seconds!

Little Andy Ant could not wait to get to school the next day! He wanted to learn how to count up to really big numbers, like how many birthdays his class would have.

One day Andy made up a new game for his friends during recess. They all got to swing on the vines!

Everyone looked up to Andy as the most fun ant in their class. "You're the best, Andy!" the children shouted.

Little Andy Ant rushed home after another fun day and told his mother, "School is the best!"

Thumbelina

From the adaptation by Lynne Suesse
Illustrated by Jane Maday

Once there was a kind woman who lived all alone in the woods. She felt lucky to be surrounded by the beauty of nature. Her only wish was for a child to share her joy.

One day, a kind old witch passed by. "I know you want a child more than anything," said the witch. "I can help you." The witch pulled a tiny bag out of her cloak. "This magic tulip bulb will make your wish come true!"

The woman planted the bulb at once. Within moments, a beautiful flower popped out of the soil.

When the woman sniffed the delicate blossom, the petals burst open. Sitting in the center of the flower was a beautiful little child.

"Why, you are no bigger than my thumb! I will call you Thumbelina." The woman knew she would love the little girl as her own.

One day, a toad heard Thumbelina singing a sweet song. The toad decided that Thumbelina should marry her son. The toad stole Thumbelina and placed her on a lily pad in the middle of a stream.

"Stay here while I get my son," demanded the toad as she dove under the water.

"Oh, I don't want to be a toad's wife!" wailed Thumbelina.

As she cried, three fish swam by and took pity on Thumbelina. They nibbled at the stem of the lily pad until it broke free.

Thumbelina sailed swiftly down the stream, and soon she reached the bank. She was tired from her adventure. A butterfly helped her weave blades of grass into a sturdy hammock.

Another butterfly carried a leaf up to make a pillow for Thumbelina's pretty head.

43

Thumbelina missed her mother very much, but she could not find her way home. Soon the weather began to get cold. Thumbelina knew she had to find a warm place to live. Luckily, she met a friendly mouse who invited Thumbelina to stay.

One day, Thumbelina and the mouse heard a strange noise. It was a sparrow who had hurt his wing and could not fly. They invited him inside.

The sparrow was surprised to see such a tiny person.

"Are you a fairy?" asked the sparrow.

44

"What is a fairy?" asked Thumbelina.

"When my wing is better, I will show you," said the sparrow.

That winter, while the mouse sewed and the sparrow rested, Thumbelina sang to pass the time. The mouse and the sparrow even made her a singing stage from a thimble the mouse had found outside her house.

When spring arrived, the sparrow's wing felt as good as new. He offered to take Thumbelina home to her mother. Thumbelina and the sparrow thanked the mouse for her kindness, and they flew away.

Soon the sparrow landed in an enchanted grove.

"This isn't where I live," said Thumbelina, confused.

Just then, a tiny boy stepped out from the petals of a big white flower. He was the prince of the fairies!

Thumbelina

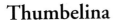

The prince took one look at Thumbelina and knew he must have her for his bride.

"I will marry you," said Thumbelina, "if you come and live in my mother's garden. I miss her so!"

The sparrow took the tiny prince and princess to the woman's garden. The woman was thrilled to find not only her beloved daughter, but also a new little son-in-law!

The sparrow visited every summer, and they all lived happily ever after.

Little Red Riding Hood

Adapted by Lisa Harkrader
Illustrated by Wendy Edelson

Once upon a time there was a little rabbit who always wore a bright red cloak with a hood. Her name was Little Red Riding Hood.

One day Little Red Riding Hood and her mother packed a basket full of good things to eat. They filled it with her grandmother's favorite foods, like carrots, orange blossom honey, and homemade breads and tarts.

"Take this basket straight to your grandmother's house," said Little Red Riding Hood's mother.

Then with a kiss on the forehead, her mother sent Little Red Riding Hood off through the woods to Grandmother's house.

Little Red Riding Hood had not gone far when a wolf approached her. "Where are you going?" he asked.

"I'm not supposed to talk to strangers," said Little Red Riding Hood.

The wolf looked at her basket. "A picnic?" he asked.

"It's not a picnic," said Little Red Riding Hood as she held the basket close. "It's a basket for my grandmother."

The wolf sniffed the basket to find out what was inside. "No flowers?" asked the wolf. "I would never visit my grandmother without a big bunch of flowers. Perhaps you should stop and pick some for her."

Little Red Riding Hood thought that was a good idea. She picked buttercups and daisies, while the wolf ran down the path toward Grandmother's house.

Grandmother was rocking in her favorite rocker, mending her favorite apron. She did not hear the door creak open. She paid careful attention to her needlework, so she did not see the big, hairy wolf sneak into her little house.

The wolf slipped into a closet and waited until he was sure that Grandmother was alone in the house. "Grrr!" snarled the wolf as he sprang from the closet.

"Oh my!" cried Grandmother as she jumped up from her chair and knocked over the table. Grandmother ran out of that house as fast as she could.

The wolf looked through Grandmother's closet and found her nightcap, gown, and some glasses. He put them on, leaped into bed, and pulled the covers up over his nose. Little Red Riding Hood arrived a few minutes later.

"Grandmother, are you home?" she called from the open door.

"In here, my little dumpling," the wolf said softly.

Little Red Riding Hood hurried inside. "Grandmother, what big ears you have!" she said as the nightcap slipped off the wolf's head.

"All the better to hear you with, my dear," said the sneaky wolf. Then Grandmother's glasses slipped down from the wolf's eyes.

"Grandmother, what big eyes you have!" said Little Red Riding Hood.

"All the better to see you with, my dear," said the wolf as he slowly pulled the covers down from his face.

"Oh Grandmother!" said Little Red Riding Hood. "What big teeth you have!"

"All the better to eat you with, my dear!" growled the wolf as he jumped off the bed.

"You're not my grandmother!" screamed Little Red Riding Hood. "Why, you're the big, bad wolf from the forest! What have you done with my grandmother?"

The wolf chuckled. "You will never find out, my dear," he said.

"That's what you think," said someone behind them. Little Red Riding Hood and the wolf turned around. There was Grandmother standing in the doorway with a big, strong lumberjack.

The wolf chuckled again. "One old lumberjack cannot catch a quick and smart wolf like me."

The wolf leaped toward the bedroom window. But he did not get very far.

Little Red Riding Hood quickly grabbed the wolf's tail, while Grandmother snatched her nightcap and pulled it down over the wolf's eyes.

The lumberjack picked up the wolf and carried him off toward the river. Little Red Riding Hood and her grandmother followed closely behind to see what would happen next.

When the lumberjack finally reached the river, he set the wolf down on a big log and quickly pushed it into the water. The wolf sadly sailed away down the river.

"He doesn't look so big out there in the middle of that wide river," said Grandmother.

"He doesn't look so bad and mean when he's so far away from us," said Little Red Riding Hood.

"And he doesn't look like he will be coming back anytime soon," said the lumberjack.

With the wolf safely gone, everyone went back to Grandmother's house and enjoyed the food in the basket. As Grandmother sipped some tea, she smiled at Little Red Riding Hood.

"You are very brave," she said. "And I'm glad I'm your grandmother."

From that day on, Little Red Riding Hood never had to worry about the wolf when she traveled through the woods to Grandmother's house.

The Wild Swans

From the adaptation by Brian Conway
Illustrated by Kathy Mitchell

Once there was a king who had three fine sons and a sweet daughter named Elise. One day the king hurried to Elise with terrible news.

"Your brothers have been taken away from us," he told her. "I know not where. I cannot stand to lose you, too."

The king told Elise to go with his most trusted servants, who would take her to safety in their home in the forest.

Elise lived hidden away for many years. When she was old enough, she set off in search of her brothers. She had no idea where to look, but she knew in her heart they were still alive, and something inside told her they needed her help.

After several days of wandering and searching, Elise met an old woman.

"Have you seen three princes?" asked Elise.

"No, but I have seen three white swans with golden crowns on their heads," the old woman replied. She showed Elise where she had seen them.

Just then, as the sun was setting, Elise looked up to see three majestic swans. They landed beside her and changed magically into three princes. Elise was overjoyed to see her brothers. They told her that an evil sorcerer had cast a spell that turned them into swans during the day. At nightfall, the moonlight made them human again. The sorcerer had also imprisoned their dear father. Elise had escaped to safety just in time.

Elise promised to do whatever she could to break the sorcerer's wicked spell. And they all vowed to find their father and free him.

That night, a fairy came to Elise in a dream. "Only you can free your brothers," the fairy whispered. "But you must sacrifice greatly.

"You must craft three shirts from the petals of roses," continued the fairy. "When you cover the swans with these shirts, the spell will be broken. But you must not open your mouth to eat, drink, or speak until the shirts are made. If you do, your brothers will be swans forever."

Elise awoke with a start to find the cave in which she slept was surrounded with hundreds of lovely rosebushes. She set to work immediately.

Elise worked day and night for thirty days. Her brothers visited her at the cave each night, and searched for their father during the day.

Elise didn't dare speak to tell them what she was doing. They cried for her pain and understood that she worked to help them.

At long last, weak and starved, Elise completed the third shirt. With barely the energy to lift even one rose petal, she summoned her last bit of strength to drape the shirts over her swan brothers. Before her eyes, the swans became men again. Elise fell into her brothers' arms and, in a faint voice, explained how the spell had been broken. "Now if only we had Father back," she whispered.

What the dream-fairy had not told Elise was that her sacrifice was powerful enough to rob the sorcerer of all his power. The sorcerer's evil could not withstand a love as great as Elise's— a love so great that she had risked her own life to save her brothers. Their father was instantly freed!

Once reunited, the happy family thrived again, and never parted from one another for the rest of their days.

Little Red Hen

Adapted by Jennifer Boudart
Illustrated by Linda Dockey Graves

The little red hen lived next to the road by the farmer's house. She shared her home with her five baby chicks and her friends, the dog, the cat, and the duck. The little red hen worked very hard. She kept the house and the yard neat and clean. Everyone liked having a clean house and good food on the table.

When it came time to do the chores, though, the other animals always seemed to disappear. The little red hen did all the work herself.

One day, the little red hen found some kernels of wheat. She showed them to the dog, the cat, and the duck and asked, "Who will help me plant these?" Her three friends looked at the little red hen.

"Not I," said the dog.

"Not I," said the cat.

"Not I," said the duck.

"Then I'll plant them myself," the little red hen told them. Soon her baby chicks came by and told her they wanted to help. The little chicks had lots of fun digging in the dirt.

After a short time they had planted all the kernels. The little red hen visited the garden every day to watch the wheat grow.

One day, she saw many weeds growing in the garden. She found her three friends leaning against the farmer's barn. The little red hen said, "Will you help me pull the weeds?"

"I can't," said the cat. "They're all dirty."

The dog said, "I need to take a nap."

The duck just quacked and waddled off to the pond.

"I'll just do it myself," said the little red hen. Then she walked back to the garden. Once again, her chicks joined her and helped her pull the weeds.

A few days later the little red hen worried that the wheat needed more water. She looked for her friends and found them on a pile of hay. The hen said, "Who will help me water the garden?"

The dog, the cat, and the duck looked down at her. "We're busy writing a song and can't be bothered now," said the dog.

"I'll just water it myself," said the little red hen. She took her watering pail to the garden, and her five chicks came to keep her company. For fun, the little red hen sprinkled the chicks with water. Before long, the whole garden had been watered while everyone played.

The summer sun shined almost every day, and the wheat grew fast. Soon it was fall, and the wheat turned golden brown. The little red hen knew what that meant. She found her friends playing cards. The hen asked, "Who will help me harvest the wheat?"

"Not I!" said the dog. "I have good cards."

"Not I!" said the cat. "I'm the dealer."

"Not I!" said the duck. "Wheat makes me sneeze."

"Then I'll harvest it and take it to the mill myself," said the little red hen. She went to the garden, and this time the five chicks were waiting for her. They all cut the wheat together.

Then they took the wheat to the mill. There the friendly miller ground the wheat into flour.

Even though she had already spent a great deal of time and energy on the garden, the little red hen knew there was still a lot more work to be done. She often told her young chicks that if a job was worth doing, it was worth doing well.

The next morning, the little red hen went outside. Her friends were sunbathing on the roof. She called to them, "Who will help me bake bread with my flour?"

The dog, the cat, and the duck did not even bother to look down at the little red hen.

"Not I!" said the dog. "It's a beautiful day. Who wants to be indoors baking bread?"

"Not I!" said the cat. "I have sunbathing to do."

"Not I!" said the duck. "All that flour will get my nice feathers dusty, and I just went swimming!"

The little red hen shook her head. She told the three, "I'll bake it myself," and then she went inside. Her chicks helped her shape the dough into a big loaf.

Soon the smell of baking bread floated in the air. The dog, the cat, and the duck came and looked into the kitchen. The chicks danced around the little red hen. "Who will help me eat this tasty, fresh bread?" asked the little red hen.

"I will!" said the dog, whose tongue was hanging out.

"I will!" said the cat, who licked her whiskers.

"I will!" said the duck, who just stared at the bread.

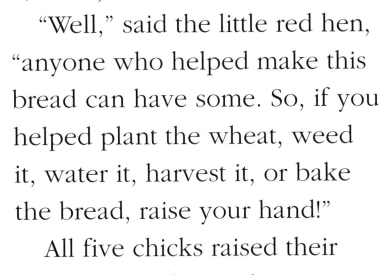

"Well," said the little red hen, "anyone who helped make this bread can have some. So, if you helped plant the wheat, weed it, water it, harvest it, or bake the bread, raise your hand!"

All five chicks raised their little wings. That night, six tummies got their fill of bread as a reward for work well done. But the dog, the cat, and the duck were left in the yard, where they could feast only on the wonderful smells.

The Five Brothers

Adapted by Brian Conway
Illustrated by Leanne Mebust

Once there were five brothers who looked exactly alike. They lived with their mother in a little house beside the sea. Their father had been a sorcerer, and the five brothers came to have very special abilities, too.

The first brother could slurp up the whole sea and hold it in his mouth. His skill was most useful when it came time for fishing.

One morning the king wanted to go swimming. But he quickly discovered the water was missing!

"Who has taken the water away?" the king said to his guards. "Go and find him!"

When the first brother saw the king's guards approaching, he quickly tried to put the water back in its place, while his brothers hurried home with their fish.

"How dare you take all of the sea for yourself!" the king scolded. "You will be punished!"

The king ordered his guards to blindfold the first brother, take him deep into the woods, and leave him there. "Please, Your Highness," said the first brother, "allow me to go and bid my dear mother good-bye."

"It is only fair," the king agreed.

The first brother went home and asked the second brother to go back in his place. The guards covered the second brother's eyes. They led him for many miles through the woods, twisting and turning away from any paths, around tree after tree. Then they left him in the forest by himself.

The second brother, who could see through the back of his head, knew exactly where he was and how to get back. Walking home, though, he ran into the guards again. They quickly grabbed him and took him to the king.

"You are clever," said the king, "but I know what to do with you."

The king ordered the guards to lock the second brother inside a box and carry him by buggy to another kingdom. "Please, Your Highness," the second brother pleaded, "allow me to go and bid my dear mother good-bye."

"It is only fair," said the king.

The second brother went home and asked the third brother to go back in his place. The third brother, who could creep through any crack, was locked in a box that was put onto a buggy. As the buggy drove off, standing right there behind two guards was the third brother!

The guards grabbed him and brought him before their king. "I know what to do with you!" growled the king. He ordered his guards to take the third brother out to sea and drop him in the deepest waters.

"Please, Your Highness," said the third brother, "allow me to go and bid my dear mother good-bye."

"It is only fair," said the king. The third brother went home and asked the fourth brother to go back in his place. The guards took the fourth brother to the deepest waters and dropped him in.

The fourth brother could stretch and stretch his legs.

He did just that until his feet touched the bottom of the sea. The fourth brother did not sink! The guards pulled him out of the water and took him to the king. "Take him to the dungeon!" the king shouted.

"Please, Your Highness," the fourth brother pleaded, "just let me go and bid my dear mother good-bye."

"I suppose it is only fair," said the king.

The fourth brother went home and asked the fifth brother to go back in his place. The guards put the fifth brother into the cold dungeon. The fifth brother could spin faster than a top, and he flew up, up, up through the roof above him.

The king was in his bed when the floor began to rumble. The frightened king gasped as the fifth brother came spinning up through the floor!

"How did you do that?" the startled king asked. "You 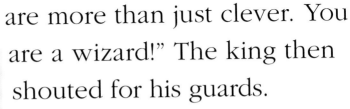 are more than just clever. You are a wizard!" The king then shouted for his guards.

"Please, Your Highness," the fifth brother pleaded. "I am different, it is true. But I have a gift, just like you." The fifth brother pointed at the king's feet.

"What do you mean?" asked the curious king. The king had very large feet, and he was very embarrassed about them.

"Why, your grand feet can be used for a very, very important job in the kingdom, Your Highness," the fifth brother replied. "Making mashed potatoes!"

The king realized that he, too, was able to do something that no one else could do. In minutes, he could make hundreds of pounds of mashed potatoes with his huge feet.

From then on, the king happily showed off his feet each day as he walked barefoot through his kingdom. The five brothers and their mother were happy too. They enjoyed a lifetime supply of mashed potatoes.

Birthday Cake Mix-Up

Written by Lisa Harkrader
Illustrated by Sherry Neidigh

Barry Bumblebee sat straight up in bed. He rubbed his eyes and looked out the window.

Oh no!" cried Barry. "The sun is up! I'm going to be late for work!"

Barry was the owner of the Busy Bee Bakery. Barry had to go to work before most bugs in town were even awake. The bakery made the most delicious baked goods in town.

Barry pulled on his white apron and baker's hat. Then he rushed out the door of his house.

When Barry arrived at the bakery, his helpers were already busy. Two bees sifted flour while another bee measured cinnamon for a batch of sticky buns. Three other bees mixed batter for the blueberry muffins. "I see we have cherry popovers in the oven," Barry said to his helpers.

Barry continued, "The only things left to make are raisin bread and chocolate chip cookies. I will make those myself."

Barry reached in his pocket for his glasses, but they were not there. "Oh no!" cried Barry. "Now where did I leave my glasses?"

The bakery would be opening soon. There was no time for Barry to look for his glasses!

"I bake things every day," said Barry. "Maybe I don't need my glasses."

Barry set out two mixing bowls. He measured the ingredients for cookies with one hand and mixed bread batter with another. Then he poured some raisins into the bread batter and some chocolate chips into the cookie dough. Now it all was ready for the oven.

Soon the oven timer dinged, and Barry squinted at the clock. "Time to take my goodies out of the oven and open the Busy Bee Bakery," said Barry.

Carla and Casey Cricket were the first to arrive at the bakery. "You are just in time to taste some freshly baked treats," said Barry as he gave Carla a slice of bread and handed Casey a cookie.

"Yum," said Carla Cricket. "I've never had chocolate chip bread before."

"I love raisin cookies," said Casey Cricket.

"Oh no! I mixed up the ingredients!" cried Barry.

"Don't worry, Barry," said Carla. "These are very delicious treats!"

"Thank you," said Barry. "That makes me feel much better. Now I need to bake a birthday cake for my niece Bibi."

Barry pulled out his cookbook. He squinted at Bibi's favorite cake recipe. "A crate of flour," he read from the recipe.

So Barry dumped a crate of flour into his biggest mixing bowl. "Two dozen eggs," Barry read, and he cracked two dozen eggs and mixed them into the flour. He added the rest of the ingredients, poured the batter into his biggest pan, and set it in the oven.

When the timer dinged, Barry peeked into the oven. "Oh no!" he cried. "This cake is huge! I should have used two eggs, not two dozen, and a cup of flour, not a crate!"

86

Birthday Cake Mix-Up

The bees frosted the cake and set it on a cart. Barry rolled the giant cake to Bibi's house. When he arrived, Barry said, "Bibi, I'm sorry."

"For what?" said Bibi as she gave her uncle a big hug. "This is the most wonderful birthday cake I've ever seen!" Bibi's guests began to clap, and Barry sighed with relief. Then Bibi gave her uncle a surprise. "I found your glasses," she said. "I hope you didn't need them at work today!"

The Emperor's New Clothes

From the adaptation by Mary Rowitz
Illustrated by John Kanzler

Once upon a time, there was a vain emperor who loved clothes more than anything else. The emperor's clothes filled all the closets and rooms in the royal palace.

The emperor also spent a lot of money on mirrors. He thought his fancy clothes made him look quite dashing, so he spent most of his free time looking at himself.

Word of the emperor who loved fine clothes reached two thieves in a faraway land. The clever thieves thought of a plan.

The thieves dressed up as traveling tailors and journeyed to the emperor's palace. They told the palace guards that they had rare and wonderful fabrics to show the emperor.

The thieves were welcomed and taken straight into the throne room.

The thieves told the emperor that their magical fabric was invisible to fools.

Then the thieves opened their bag and pretended to lift something.

The emperor squinted. He saw nothing at all! *I must be a fool!* he thought.

The emperor was very embarrassed, so he said, "That fabric is magnificent! I will offer you twenty pieces of gold to make me a suit with it."

The thieves, delighted, took the emperor's measurements and set to work.

After a few days, the royal minister went to see how the suit was coming along. He found the tailors cutting away at the air with their scissors and sewing up fabric that was not there!

I cannot see any fabric! Could it be that I am a fool? gulped the minister.

"Say, minister," said the thief, "order us some more food, would you? All this hard work makes us hungry."

That much must be true, the minister thought. The thieves had eaten so much already. They must be working hard on something!

The minister hurried off to report back to the emperor.

"Your Majesty, the tailors are hard at work on your suit," he said. The minister did not want to appear foolish, so he added, "It is simply divine!"

At long last, the thieves brought the emperor his new suit, and he put it on.

The emperor was standing in front of a mirror wearing only his underwear, admiring a new suit that wasn't even there!

The emperor called for a royal parade the next day. He wanted to show off his new suit to everyone in the land.

At the parade, everyone pushed and shoved to get the best view. The people had heard that fools could not see the magical fabric, and they wanted to find out who amongst them was a fool.

No one would admit that they couldn't see the emperor's suit. Nobody wanted to look like a fool.

Suddenly a boy cried out, "The emperor is wearing nothing but his underwear!"

Everyone in the crowd began to laugh. They had all been foolish. They pretended to see a suit that was not even there, because they were afraid of what others would think.

The embarrassed emperor rushed back to the palace to put on some clothes.

Then he invited the honest boy to speak with him. "I hereby proclaim you a junior minister," said the emperor. "You have proven your courage and bravery by telling the truth when no one else would!"

The Velveteen Rabbit

Based on the original story by Margery Williams
Adapted by Cynthia Benjamin and Megan Musgrave
Illustrated by Phil Bliss and Jim Bliss

One bright Easter morning, a little boy woke up to find a wonderful basket in his playroom. He was very excited! The basket was full of chocolate eggs and marshmallow treats. But the best present of all was his new velveteen rabbit.

The rabbit's coat was soft, and the insides of its ears were shiny satin. The boy played with his rabbit all day. Soon it was time for dinner, and the boy had to leave his rabbit in the playroom.

Once the boy was gone, the other toys talked to the rabbit.

"I can walk back and forth," said a shiny robot. "Someday I am going to be real. Are you?"

The rabbit turned to Old Horse. He was the oldest and wisest toy in the playroom. "What's real?" asked the rabbit.

"Real is when a child loves you very much for a long, long time," said Old Horse. "It is when he hugs you so much that your shiny coat grows dull and you do not look so new anymore. When you are real you do not care how you look because there is nothing better than being loved."

Soon the boy came back into the playroom.

"Come on, Bunny," said the boy. "It's bedtime." The boy took the rabbit to bed with him and snuggled him close all night. The rabbit felt very warm and cozy.

"This must be what it feels like to be loved," thought the rabbit. "Someday I am going to be real."

One day the boy put the rabbit in his red wagon. "You seem to like that rabbit better than all your other toys," said the boy's mother.

"He's not a toy, he's real," said the boy. The rabbit was so happy to hear this. "The boy really loves me," thought the rabbit. "And now I am real."

The boy soon took the velveteen rabbit on a ride to the woods. When the boy left the rabbit to search for treasures, two furry creatures came out from behind the trees. "What are you?" one of the creatures asked the velveteen rabbit.

"I'm a rabbit, just like you!" said the velveteen rabbit.

"Then why can't you move like this?" asked one of the other rabbits as he hopped around. "You're not real."

"Yes I am," said the velveteen rabbit. "The boy told me so." The other rabbits just giggled and hopped away.

As time passed, the velveteen rabbit's fur wore away from being hugged by the boy so much. But the rabbit was happy because he knew the boy loved him.

One day, though, the boy became sick. The doctor told the boy's parents, "You must take your son to the seaside so he can rest and get better."

The boy did not want the velveteen rabbit to get sick, too, so before he went away he left the rabbit under their favorite tree in the woods. "I want you to always remember the wonderful times we had together, Bunny," the boy said sadly.

When the boy went away, the rabbit became very sad, too. He was so sad that he began to cry. A real tear slid down his velveteen cheek.

Suddenly, as the rabbit looked down, a flower grew out of the spot where his tear had fallen.

The blue petals of the flower slowly opened, and out flew a beautiful fairy.

"Do not cry, little rabbit," said the fairy. "I am the fairy of playroom magic. When toys have been loved by a child as much as the boy loved you, I make them real."

"Wasn't I already real?" asked the velveteen rabbit.

"You were real only to the boy because he loved you so much," said the fairy. "Now, because you have been so kind to the boy, and because you truly love him, I will make you real to everyone!"

With that, the fairy gently kissed the velveteen rabbit. "I can move!" cried the rabbit as he started to hop around. "This is so wonderful!"

The velveteen rabbit began to leap and jump for joy. "Now I really am real!" he said as he laughed and hopped around some more. Just then, a group of real rabbits gathered around. "Aren't you the same rabbit we saw before?" asked a brown rabbit.

"Yes I am," said the velveteen rabbit. "But now I truly am real! Watch me hop around just like all of you!"

The Velveteen Rabbit

Soon the others asked him to join their group. Away they all ran into the woods, with the velveteen rabbit smiling at his new friends.

Months later, the boy returned to the woods. Suddenly, a rabbit hopped up to him. "You're my velveteen rabbit, aren't you?" asked the boy, as the rabbit winked at him. "I always knew you were real! I will come to visit you as often as I can!"

The Goose Girl

From the adaptation by Lisa Harkrader
Illustrated by Cindy Salans Rosenheim

Once a graceful, kind princess named Elizabeth promised to marry a prince she had never met. Elizabeth watched as her belongings were loaded onto her beloved horse, Falada. Falada was a special horse, for he could speak.

The princess's mother, a kind and generous queen, chose a servant named Zelda to look after the princess. Then the queen gave Elizabeth one last gift.

"This is my royal ring," said the queen. "I want you to have it. When you arrive at your new castle, this ring will prove who you are."

Princess Elizabeth and Zelda set off for the prince's kingdom. Elizabeth rode faithful Falada, and Zelda rode a sure-footed old mare.

After a few miles, Princess Elizabeth grew thirsty. She knelt on the bank of a stream to drink. As she drank, her mother's ring slid from her finger, but Elizabeth did not notice. Zelda waded into the stream and fetched it.

Elizabeth was brushing the mud from her gown when she saw the ring was gone. "Oh, no!" she cried.

Zelda held up the ring. "Is this what you're looking for, Princess?"

"Thank goodness! Zelda, you've saved me," said a grateful Elizabeth.

"This time, perhaps." Zelda slid the ring onto her own finger. "But what about next time? I should keep this for you. And after what just happened, I think I should ride Falada and keep an eye on your possessions."

"You're right," said the princess. "You're too good to me."

After switching clothes and horses, Elizabeth and Zelda set off once more.

At the castle, the king was waiting.

"Show me to my room and send up some food," said Zelda. "I'm tired and hungry."

The king was surprised at Zelda's rudeness, but he said politely, "We are delighted that you've arrived safely, Princess." He turned to Elizabeth. "We'll find a room for you and send you a hot meal."

"Thank you, Your Majesty," said Elizabeth. "But I'm the princess."

Zelda snorted. "You? Your clothes are rags and you were riding a swayback mare." Zelda held out her hand to show off the queen's ring. "This proves who I am. My mother gave it to me before we left."

The king sent Elizabeth off with the goose boy, Conrad. She was to be the new goose girl.

110

Each morning, Elizabeth and Conrad led the geese to a meadow. One day, Elizabeth found Falada in a pasture in the farthest corner of the kingdom.

The two old friends talked and talked. Elizabeth insisted that she and Conrad take the geese to Falada's pasture each day. Conrad grew tired of walking so far, and went to complain to the king.

"She talks to that horse all day," said Conrad, "and the horse just tells her that a princess should not be tending geese." Curious, the king went to the pasture. The talking horse revealed that Elizabeth was indeed the true princess!

That very night, the king declared that Zelda would be the goose girl from then on. He now knew that he should have recognized a true princess by her goodness and grace, not by her fine clothes and jewels.

Little Witch

Written by Brian Conway
Illustrated by Leanne Mebust

Little Wanda Witch kept busy studying her big book of magic spells. But she really wanted to play the day away like the other witches did.

Wanda also wanted the other witches to like her. They were older than she was, but they were the only witches to play with. Wanda thought that if she learned all of her witch spells, she could be more like them. Magic spells are never easy, even for a smart little witch like Wanda.

"Abracadabble!" said Wanda. "No, that's not it. Abracabubble! No, that's not right either." Sometimes the spells made Wanda dizzy.

The book was full of tricky tongue-twisting talk. But Wanda was not the kind of witch who gave up easily. Wanda knew she could learn every last trick in that big book of spells.

"Someday," Wanda thought, "I'll be big enough to boil and bubble and all that stuff." And sure enough, Wanda soon was ready for her first witch's trick.

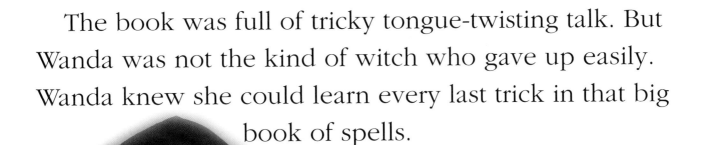

Wanda had practiced the trick over and over again in her mind. Now she would do it for real!

Wanda looked at her book one last time. Then she hopped on one foot and twiddled her fingers, just like her big book of magic spells said. Finally, Wanda began to chant.

"Broom, broom, who needs you? Warty, haggy witches do. You can sweep the floors inside. A tricycle's the thing to ride!"

Wanda felt some magic stirring in the air. She twiddled her fingers again, passing a zap from her hands to the broom.

POOF! It worked! Well, sort of. The broom changed, but not like Wanda wanted it to.

"Oops!" said a disappointed Wanda. "That's not a tricycle. It's an icicle!"

Wanda went back to her book of spells to study some more. "I wonder what went wrong?" said Wanda to her kitten. Wanda looked at her book. "I did everything right. It's the spell that must be wrong."

So Wanda found another spell she could try right away. "I need your help, Kitty," said Wanda. Kitty tried to hide under the table. Kitty liked being a kitty. She did not want to turn into an icicle or a spider.

"Don't worry, Kitty," Wanda assured her. "It's an easy one. Now just stay still."

Just to be safe, Wanda read right from the book this time. In her very best witch's voice, Wanda shrieked, "Abracablue and abracablots! Wouldn't Kitty be pretty with polka-dot spots?"

POOF! This trick worked too, but not like Wanda thought it would. Wanda got lots of spots, it's true, but they were not on her kitten. They were on the polka-dotted puppy dogs all over her bedroom!

Wanda had some troubles, but she would never give up. She shooed the puppies out to some polka-dotted doghouses in the yard, and then she found a toad.

This toad did not have a single wart on his entire body. Wanda felt sorry for the little guy. She knew she had a spell to get his skin as lumpy as it should be.

Wanda clicked her heels, pointed at the toad, and chanted her spell. "Dimples and pimples and bumps of all sorts. A toad's needs are simple — clumps of big warts!"

POOF! Wanda's magic gently zapped the toad. When she saw what had happened, Wanda could not believe her eyes!

Could it be true? Yes! Wanda's spell worked! She hurried out to the cauldron to show the other witches her happy toad.

"I did it! I did it!" Wanda called to the other witches. "It's my first real witch's trick. Look at how lumpy the toad is now."

"Oooh, what marvelous warts," the other witches cooed. "We must have some."

So Wanda tried her wonderful wart trick on the other witches. She knew what had worked the first time, so she did not change a thing this time around.

POOF! The spell worked again! The other witches now had lots and lots of lumpy warts.

But suddenly they were not witches anymore. They had turned into toads! "Uh-oh," Wanda sighed.

Then Kitty brought Wanda her little witch's broom. Wanda finally remembered the first rule of witchery! It was not in any book. Wanda learned it from her mother when she was very small.

"If you find you're in a mess, your little witch's broom's the best. For fixing messes clean and clear, just wave your broom around, my dear!"

Wanda did just that. *POOF*! The warty toads became witches again! And the witches were not mad at Wanda at all. In fact, they thought Wanda was the smartest little witch around.

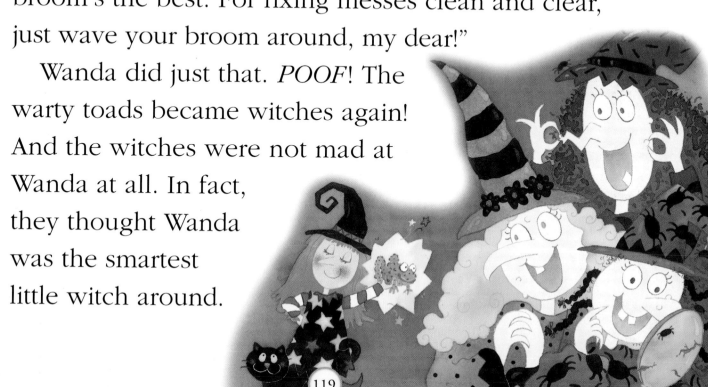

The Frog Prince

From the adaptation by Anne H. Foley
Illustrated by Judy Love

Once upon a time, there lived a young princess who loved nothing more than to play with her favorite golden ball. One afternoon, she threw the golden ball a little too far, and it fell into a deep pond.

The princess peered into the water and saw her lovely ball sparkling all the way at the bottom. All she could do was weep over the loss of her beautiful golden ball.

Suddenly the princess heard a voice say, "What troubles you?"

The princess looked down and saw a frog. The princess had never seen a talking frog before, but she hid her surprise and answered him.

"I am crying because my golden ball is lost in the pond," she said.

The frog said, "I will rescue your golden ball, if you promise you will be my friend forever."

The princess did not want to befriend a slimy frog! She hoped he would forget his request as soon as the task was done.

"I promise," lied the princess, "that we shall be best friends."

The frog dove under the water and found the golden ball. As soon as he brought the ball to the surface, the princess snatched it up. She ran away, leaving the frog behind.

But the frog did not forget the princess's promise. That evening, the frog hopped all the way to the castle, and hopped into the dining hall as the royal family was eating dinner.

"Mmmm, I love mashed potatoes and peas!" he exclaimed, and began to eat from the princess's plate.

"Er, Princess," said the king, "why is there a frog at the dinner table?"

The princess explained the promise she had made, looking at the frog with disgust all the while.

"Whether you like the frog or not," said the stern king, "you must keep your promise to him."

Reluctantly, the princess offered her friendship—and her dinner—to the frog.

"Now I am thirsty," croaked the frog. "Water, please, Princess."

The princess remembered her promise to the frog. She poured him a glass of water, and he drank it down.

"Now for dessert! I'd like some shoofly pie," said the frog.

The princess could take no more of the frog's demands. She slammed her fist on the table. The table shook, and the frog lost his balance and fell off the table. The princess and the king leaned over the edge of the table to see what had happened to the frog. But instead of the frog, there was a handsome young prince!

"What is going on here?" asked the furious princess.

The prince explained, "An evil witch turned me into a frog. The only way I could become a prince again was to make a princess angry with me. When you appeared, I saw a chance to break the spell. Your anger has turned me back into a prince! You have saved my life."

In that brief moment, the princess and the prince fell in love and were soon married. The princess forgave the prince for deceiving her, and the prince forgave the princess for trying to break her promise.

The two agreed to be honest with one another forever more, and the joyous couple spent the rest of their days together.

Goldilocks and the Three Bears

Adapted by Jennifer Boudart
Illustrated by David Merrell

There once was a family of three bears. Papa Bear, Mama Bear, and little Baby Bear lived in a cozy cottage right in the heart of the forest.

Each day Mama Bear made three bowls of oatmeal and set them out on the table. While the oatmeal cooled, the Bear family would take a nice walk in the forest. One morning there also was a young girl walking in the forest.

126

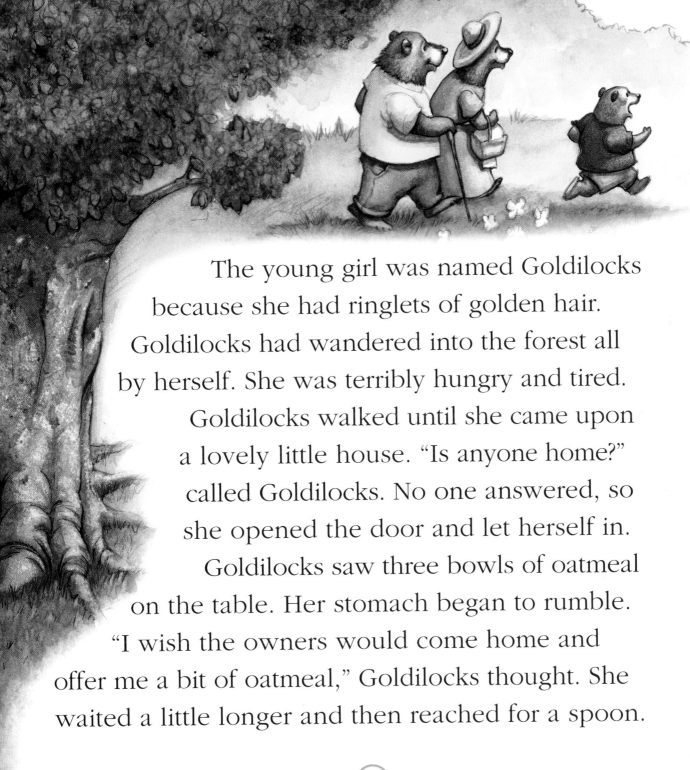

The young girl was named Goldilocks
because she had ringlets of golden hair.
Goldilocks had wandered into the forest all
by herself. She was terribly hungry and tired.
Goldilocks walked until she came upon
a lovely little house. "Is anyone home?"
called Goldilocks. No one answered, so
she opened the door and let herself in.
Goldilocks saw three bowls of oatmeal
on the table. Her stomach began to rumble.
"I wish the owners would come home and
offer me a bit of oatmeal," Goldilocks thought. She
waited a little longer and then reached for a spoon.

Goldilocks dipped the spoon into the largest bowl of oatmeal, which belonged to Papa Bear. "Oh no, this oatmeal is much too hot!" Goldilocks said. She then tried some oatmeal from the middle-size bowl that belonged to Mama Bear. "And this oatmeal is much too cold," she said.

Finally, Goldilocks took a small taste from the little bowl that was set out for Baby Bear. "This is the most perfect oatmeal ever!" she said, and she licked the bowl clean.

Goldilocks felt full after eating the oatmeal. She poked her head into another room of the house and saw three lovely chairs. Goldilocks decided to sit in the big chair that belonged to Papa Bear.

"Oh no, this chair is much too hard!" she said. Then she took a seat in the nice middle-size chair where Mama Bear enjoyed sitting. "This chair is much too soft," Goldilocks said.

Goldilocks moved on to the last chair. It was a tiny rocking chair that Baby Bear loved to rock back and forth in.

"This is the most perfect chair!" said Goldilocks as she laughed with joy.

After a while, Goldilocks tried to squeeze out of the small chair, but she was stuck. She tried to stand up again, but the chair broke into pieces beneath her.

"Oh my!" said Goldilocks. "I have broken the chair. I must wait here for the owners to come home so that I can tell them how sorry I am."

But there was no place left for Goldilocks to sit, so she wandered through the cozy cottage.

Goldilocks came across a lovely room with three beds in a row. She lay on the largest bed, which belonged to Papa Bear.

"Oh no, this bed is much too hard," Goldilocks said. Goldilocks then tried the middle-size bed where Mama Bear liked to rest all winter.

"This bed is too soft!" Goldilocks said. There was only one more bed. Goldilocks lay down in the bed where Baby Bear napped each afternoon.

"What a perfect little bed!" said Goldilocks. Within moments, Goldilocks was sleeping so soundly that she did not hear the Bear family come home.

Papa Bear, Mama Bear, and Baby Bear were ready for breakfast. When they got to the kitchen, they could not believe their eyes!

"Someone has been eating my oatmeal!" said Papa Bear in his loud, rumbly voice.

"Someone has been eating my oatmeal as well," said Mama Bear. "And that someone has left quite a mess!"

Baby Bear went to his bowl of oatmeal. "Someone has eaten *all* of my oatmeal!" cried Baby Bear.

The Bear family walked into their sitting room, and again they were surprised. "Someone has been sitting in my chair, I think!" Papa Bear said in his loud voice.

"Someone has been sitting in my chair as well," said Mama Bear. But when Baby Bear went over to his favorite rocking chair, he found it was broken to pieces.

"Oh my," Baby Bear cried. "Someone has been sitting in my chair, and that someone was very careless."

"Maybe we should check the bedroom," said Mama Bear. The Bear family walked to their bedroom.

"Someone has been sleeping in my bed," said Papa Bear. Mama Bear looked at her middle-size bed. "Someone has been sleeping in my bed too," she said. Baby Bear walked slowly to his small bed and saw what was under the covers. Frightened, he touched Goldilocks gently to see if she was real. He ran to his parents. "Someone has been sleeping in my bed," said Baby Bear. "And that someone is sleeping there still!"

Goldilocks slowly opened her eyes and saw the three bears. Screaming, Goldilocks leaped from the bed.

"Who are you?" asked Papa Bear.

Goldilocks jumped right out the window and ran straight through the forest to her home.

The Bear family would never know who she was or why she had come. Baby Bear sometimes wished she would come back and play, even if that meant sharing his oatmeal.

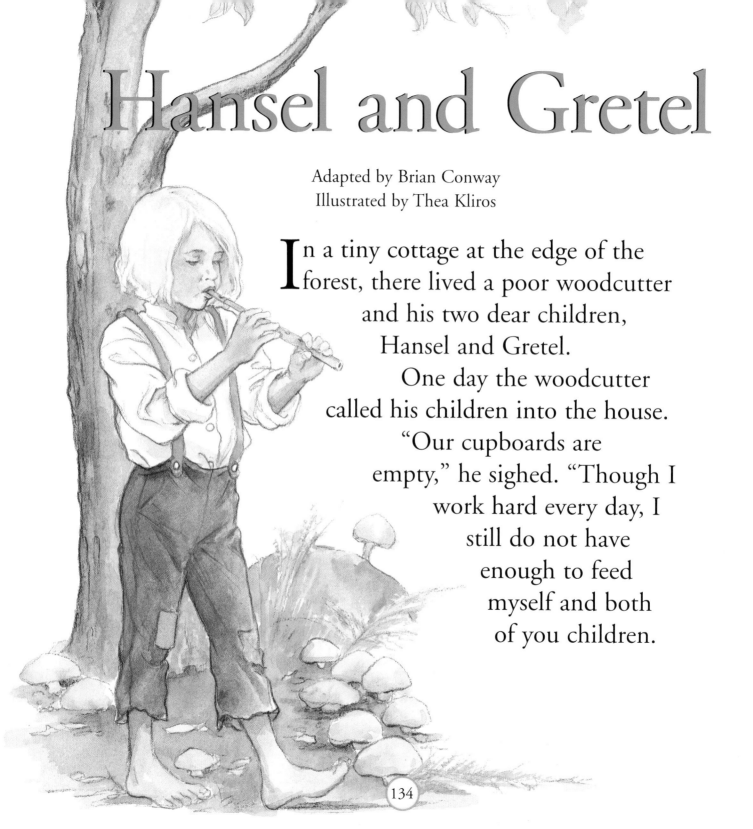

Hansel and Gretel

Adapted by Brian Conway
Illustrated by Thea Kliros

In a tiny cottage at the edge of the forest, there lived a poor woodcutter and his two dear children, Hansel and Gretel.

One day the woodcutter called his children into the house. "Our cupboards are empty," he sighed. "Though I work hard every day, I still do not have enough to feed myself and both of you children.

"I'm afraid I must teach you how to care for yourselves," he said sadly. "Tomorrow I will teach you how to hunt, fish, and gather fruit," the woodcutter concluded.

Hansel and Gretel were clever children, and wanted to make their father proud. So they made a plan to help him.

Early the next morning, the children set out into the woods without their father, hoping to bring back enough food for supper.

Hansel and Gretel dropped a trail of bread crumbs behind them as they walked. They planned to follow the trail back home.

They wandered through the woods all day long, but could find no food. Too late, the children discovered that their path of bread crumbs had been eaten up by birds. They were lost!

Suddenly, they saw a lonely little house. As they got closer, they could not believe their eyes. It was a gingerbread house, covered with sweets! The children broke pieces from the house and began to eat.

Just then the door opened, and an old woman hobbled out.

"Please excuse us," says Hansel. "But we are lost and very hungry."

"Well, well," said the old woman, peering down at the children. "Come inside and I will fix you a nice hot meal."

Hansel and Gretel followed the woman into the house. Immediately, the old woman served them hot turkey, fresh fruit, cookies, and cakes. The children ate and ate.

"Go ahead," said the woman. "Have some more."

Hansel and Gretel happily filled their plates again. The old woman held Gretel's arm and said, "My, but you are skinny. I will fatten you right up!"

Startled, Gretel said, "But I like the size I am now! Why should I be fatter?"

"All children should be plump and healthy," said the old woman with a chuckle. "I hope you two have room for some apple pie!"

Hansel and Gretel wondered why the old woman had not eaten. She was still keeping busy in the kitchen, building up the fire in the oven.

"There is just one more dish to make," she said with a scary laugh. "I will have my fill of it soon."

"I think this strange old woman is not nice at all!" whispered Hansel, worried.

"She wants us to be plump so she can put us in that oven and have us for supper!" said Gretel.

Hansel and Gretel snuck up behind the old woman, bumped her into the oven, and ran away as fast as they could!

After many days of searching, Hansel and Gretel found their way back to their father's cottage. As soon as the woodcutter saw his children, he ran to hug them.

"I've missed you both so much," he said. "I promise we'll always have enough to eat, and I will never let you out of my sight again."

Hansel and Gretel were happy to be home.

Puss in Boots

Adapted by Brian Conway
Illustrated by Victoria and Julius Lisi

Puss was a very clever cat. For a long time he belonged to an old farmer. But when the farmer died, Puss could not live on his own. He decided that he would need a new master. Puss went to see the farmer's son.

"I was quite loyal to your father," Puss said, "and he was quite fond of me. If you would be my new master, I promise to serve you just as well."

The farmer's son was very busy with his chores. He did not think he could take care of Puss, too. "If I am going to be your new master, you will have to work for me," said the young man.

"I will work very hard," said Puss. "Just give me a sack and a pair of boots," Puss told the young man, "and you will see how useful I can be."

The farmer's son found a cloth sack and an old pair of boots in the barn. "Let's see what you can do with these," he said.

Puss quickly slid into his new boots. They were sturdy and comfortable. "These will make it easy for me to hunt through the thick brush and mud in the forest," said Puss.

Puss took the empty sack and ran into the woods. "This sack will not be empty for long," Puss called back to his new master. "I will take care of you. You will see."

Before long, Puss had trapped a rabbit inside the sack. Puss carried it to the gates of the palace.

"I would like to see the king," Puss told the palace guard. "Please tell him that I have a gift for him."

Puss was calm and bold in the king's throne room. "Your Royal Highness," he said with a bow, "I offer you a gift from my master."

"What a fine rabbit!" said the king. "I receive many gifts, but this is the finest I have seen in a long time. You are an exceptional cat. Who is your master?"

Puss knew the king would not be impressed with a farmer's son. Puss made up a name, one that sounded very noble.

"My master is the Duke of Carabas," said Puss.

"The Duke of Carabas?" said the king. "I have not heard of him, but please be sure to give him my thanks."

"Indeed, I shall thank him, my king," Puss said as he waved good-bye.

Puss heard about the king's plan to take a carriage ride. The royal carriage would pass by the young man's farm. Puss also learned that the king's daughter, the beautiful princess, would join the king on his ride. Puss rushed home to his master's farm.

The young man was busy with his chores. "Hurry!" said Puss. "Take off your clothes and jump in the river!"

Puss' master was shocked. "Why should I do such a silly thing?" he asked.

"It is for the best," said Puss. "You will see." Puss then gave his master a gentle push into the river just moments before the king's carriage arrived. "Please help!" Puss cried. "The Duke of Carabas is drowning!"

The king remembered the unusual cat. He ordered his guards to stop the carriage.

"My master has been robbed!" Puss told the king. "The thieves took everything and left him to drown!"

The king ordered his guards to pull the young man from the river. Dripping wet and confused, the young man now faced the king.

"At last I meet the great Duke of Carabas," said the king. "Your charming servant has told me so much about you." Puss then bowed politely.

The farmer's son was puzzled. The king ordered one of his guards to return to the palace and bring back a royal suit for the young man. Once the young man changed into the suit, the king said, "Won't you join us on our carriage ride?"

"I would be quite honored," said the young man.

As he climbed into the carriage, the young man saw the beautiful princess. He blushed as he sat beside her.

While the royal carriage rolled along the country road, Puss was still busy with the plans he had for his new master. Puss ran up ahead to a huge castle.

A wicked giant lived in the castle. This giant had magical powers, which he used to scare his neighbors and steal their land.

No one was brave or bold enough to enter the giant's castle. But Puss was not afraid.

Puss walked into the castle and strolled right up to the giant. "What are you doing here?" the giant roared.

"I have heard that you are very powerful," Puss calmly told the giant. "But I do not believe it."

"Huh!" the giant huffed. "I am more powerful than anyone, even the king! I can become a hawk, a wolf, a lion, or a grizzly bear. I can do anything!"

"Only a very powerful giant could change himself into a tiny little mouse," said Puss.

The giant laughed. "That's easy," he said.

The giant shrunk down and became a mouse. Now Puss towered over the giant. Puss pounced on him and popped him into his mouth!

When the royal carriage rode by the castle gates, Puss called out, "Welcome to my master's home!"

"The Duke would be honored if you and your lovely daughter would stay for dinner," Puss told the king.

They all had a wonderful feast, and the princess and the young man got along splendidly at dinner. The princess whispered to her father, "I believe I would like to marry this young man, the Duke of Carabas."

There was a royal wedding the very next day. Puss had taken good care of his new master, so his master took good care of him. Puss had a fine new pair of boots, and he wore them at fancy parties and in royal parades. Exactly where a puss in boots belongs.

The Lion and the Mouse

Adapted by Sarah Toast
Illustrated by Krista Brauckmann-Towns

One day a lion was taking a nice nap in the warm sun. Nearby, a busy little mouse scurried along looking for berries. But all the berries were too high for her to reach.

Then the mouse spotted a lovely bunch of berries that she could reach by climbing on the rock below them. When she did, the mouse discovered that she had not climbed a rock at all. She had climbed right on top of the lion's head!

The lion did not like to be bothered while he was sleeping. He awoke with a loud grumble.

"Who dares to tickle my head while I'm taking a nap?" roared the lion. The mouse quickly jumped off the lion's head and started to run away.

The lion grabbed for the little mouse as quickly as he could, but she was too fast, and he just missed her. The quick little mouse hurried to get away from the lion. She zigged and zagged through the grass, but the lion was always just one step behind. At last the lion chased the mouse right back to where they had started. The poor little mouse was too tired to run anymore.

The lion scooped her up in his huge paw.

"Little mouse," roared the lion. "Don't you know that I am the king of the forest? Why did you wake me up from my pleasant nap by tickling my head?"

"Oh please, lion," said the mouse. "I was only trying to get some lovely berries."

"Just see how much you like it when I tickle your head with my big claws," said the lion.

"Please, lion," pleaded the mouse. "If you spare me, I am sure I will be able to help you someday."

The lion stopped suddenly and looked at the mouse. The lion began to smile, and then he began to laugh. "How could you, a tiny mouse, help the most powerful animal around?" he chuckled loudly. "That's so funny. I'll let you go — this time."

Then the lion laughed some more. He rolled over on his back, kicking and roaring with laughter.

The mouse had to leap out of the lion's way to avoid being crushed. Off she ran.

Still chuckling, the lion got up and realized he was hungry. He set out to find some lunch, and it was not long before he smelled food. Walking toward the good smell, the lion got caught in a trap set by hunters.

The lion was stuck in the strong ropes, and the more he wriggled and struggled, the tighter the ropes held him. Fearing the hunters would soon return, the terrified lion roared for help.

The mouse heard the lion's roars from far away. At first she was a little afraid to go back, thinking the lion might hurt her.

But the lion's cries for help made the mouse sad, and she remembered the promise she made to help him. The mouse hurried to where the lion was tangled in the trap.

"Oh lion," said the mouse. "I know what it feels like to be caught. But you do not need to worry. I will try to help you."

"I don't think there is anything you can do," said the lion. "These ropes are very strong. I have pushed and pulled with all my might, but I cannot get free."

"I have an idea!" said the mouse. "Just hold still, and I will get to work." She quickly began chewing through the thick ropes with her small, sharp teeth.

The mouse worked and worked, and before long she had chewed through enough rope for the lion to get out of the trap!

Soon the lion wriggled free. He was very grateful to the mouse. "Mouse," he said, "I thank you for saving me, and I am sorry that I laughed at you before."

"I told you that I would help you someday when you agreed to spare me," said the mouse. "I always keep my word."

Then the lion scooped up the mouse and placed her on his head. He carried her back to the berry bush and lay down under it. "Mouse," he said, "I want you to reach up and pick one of those berries that you wanted earlier today."

The mouse plucked the biggest berry she could find. The lion took the mouse off of his head and held her in his paw.

"Let's stick together," he said. "I can help you reach the berries, and you can get me out of a tight spot now and then."

"Okay!" said the mouse. "I will pick you some berries to eat, and we can have a picnic together."

"I don't know if I would like to eat berries, but just having your company would be fine with me," said the lion.

So if you are ever walking along and see a lion laughing and carrying a little mouse, you will know that these two have become great friends because they showed a great deal of kindness to one another.

Cinderella

Adapted by Amy Adair
Illustrated by Kathi McCord

Once upon a time, there was a sweet, kind, and pretty young girl named Cinderella. She had a very mean stepmother and two stepsisters who made her life miserable. They all treated Cinderella as if she were a mere servant.

Cinderella worked hard all day while her stepmother and stepsisters spent their days preening in front of the mirror. But her heart was so pure, she didn't even mind.

One day, something very exciting arrived. It was an invitation to the prince's fancy ball! But Cinderella was not allowed to go.

Finally, it was the night of the ball. As the stepmother and her daughters climbed into their coach and rode off to the ball, Cinderella began to cry. "Why must I stay at home and sweep up the hearth while everyone else goes to the ball? Am I not as good and kind as everyone else?" cried Cinderella to herself.

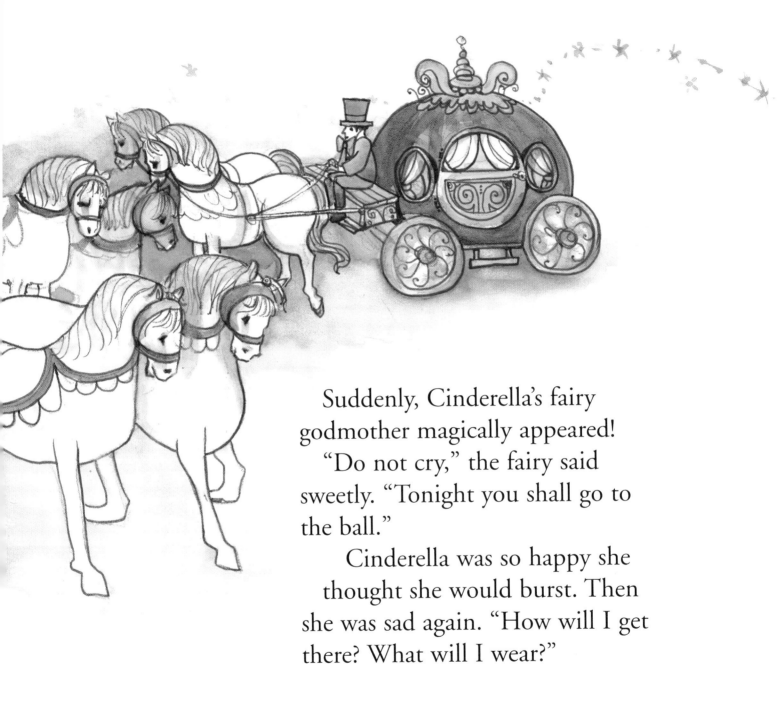

Suddenly, Cinderella's fairy godmother magically appeared!

"Do not cry," the fairy said sweetly. "Tonight you shall go to the ball."

Cinderella was so happy she thought she would burst. Then she was sad again. "How will I get there? What will I wear?"

With a wave of her wand, the fairy godmother turned an ordinary pumpkin into a lavish coach. Poof! The fairy godmother transformed six white mice into strong white horses, and changed a rat into a handsome driver.

Finally, the fairy godmother waved her wand, and Cinderella's old dress turned into a lovely gown, complete with delicate glass slippers.

As Cinderella stepped into her coach, her fairy godmother called out a warning. "At midnight, the coach will turn back into a pumpkin, the horses into mice, the driver into a rat. You must not be late!"

When Cinderella arrived at the ball, the prince fell in love with her at first sight. He would dance with no one else. As they glided across the floor, Cinderella fell in love with the prince, too.

Cinderella was so happy, she forgot the time. When the clock sounded the ninth stroke of midnight, Cinderella remembered her fairy godmother's warning and dashed out of the ballroom! Cinderella flew down the palace steps in such a hurry, she left one of her glass slippers behind.

The prince ran after Cinderella, but it was too late. She was already gone. He had never even learned her name!

The prince spied the glass slipper on the palace steps. It must belong to her, he thought. He vowed to find the slipper's mysterious owner.

The very next day, the prince began to search for the maiden who could wear the glass slipper. He visited every home in the land. Finally, the prince arrived at Cinderella's house.

The stepsisters both tried on the slipper. They pulled and tugged and pushed, but their feet were just too big.

Cinderella asked softly, "May I try?" The prince held out the glass slipper for Cinderella. Her foot slipped into it with ease!

"It fits!" shrieked the stepmother.

"It fits!" howled the stepsisters.

"It fits!" whispered the prince.

He was so overcome with love and joy that he and Cinderella were married that very day! They lived happily ever after.

As for the stepmother and stepsisters, Cinderella did not punish them. But they did have to learn how to do their own cooking, cleaning, and ironing. And that was punishment enough.

The Pied Piper of Hamelin

Adapted by Carolyn Quattrocki
Illustrated by Tim Ellis

Once upon a time, far away and long ago, there was a town called Hamelin. It was a pleasant little town with a river on one side and a high mountain on the other.

One day the people of Hamelin saw that they had a serious problem. Their lovely town was full of rats! Rats were in the trees, the streets, the alleys, the attics, and the cellars. In short, rats were practically everywhere!

Rats went into the kitchens and bothered the cooks. They fought with the dogs and bit the cats. They were so noisy that ladies having their tea together could scarcely hear each other. What on earth were the poor people of Hamelin to do?

The most important man in town was the mayor. He wore a cape made of fine silk and a matching hat. It was his job to see that everything in town ran smoothly.

The mayor had a town council to help him. The mayor and the council met each week at the town hall to talk about all the things that needed to be done. The meetings were festive occasions, and there was always a feast of good food and wine.

One day the townspeople said to themselves, "We have had enough of these rats in our town! The mayor and his council sit and do nothing while the rats are  running around everywhere. Something must be done about this!"

Soon a large group of people gathered in front of the town hall and cried out, "Let us see the mayor!"

In his office the mayor listened to the people's complaints. He knew how awful it was to have rats everywhere in town. But the mayor and his council did not have the slightest idea of how to fix the problem.

Suddenly there was a knock at the mayor's door. The people all turned to see a strange fellow standing there as the door opened. He was wearing a long red cape and a hat with a red feather. He had yellow hair, and a pipe hung from a silk scarf around his neck.

"I am a poor piper," the man said, "but I can rid your town of rats. Would you pay me a hundred pieces of gold to do it?"

"Oh, I would give a thousand pieces of gold to anyone who could rid us of these rats!" exclaimed the mayor. The members of the town council shouted, "Yes, yes! A thousand pieces of gold!"

The pied piper
bowed and then walked
to the town square.

As the pied piper began to
play, everyone was amazed at how beautiful and
sweet the music sounded! Then suddenly, rats came
running toward the pied piper from all directions. Big
rats, small rats, thin rats, fat rats, old rats, and young
rats all came running. Before long, the pied piper had
a whole army of rats marching behind him.

Through the town and to the edge of the river the
rats followed the pied piper. At the river's edge he
paused, but the rats kept going. Without stopping,
every single rat jumped into the river and drowned.

Everyone was astonished. All the rats were gone! The people cheered as the pied piper walked back to the town hall.

"I have come to collect my thousand pieces of gold," the pied piper said to the mayor.

"But sir!" cried the mayor. "That was only a joke! You cannot expect us to pay a thousand pieces of gold for such short work. Here are twenty-five pieces."

"You promised one thousand," said the pied piper.

"All right, here are fifty pieces," said the mayor. "Take them and be gone."

The pied piper became angry. The mayor and the town council had lied to him, and he did not like that at all. The pied piper decided to teach them a lesson. He began to play his pipe again as he walked to the town square.

This time the children of the town heard the music and came running toward the pied piper from all directions. The beautiful music was so sweet to their ears that they could not help themselves.

Little hands clapped to the music. Small feet danced to the merry tune. What a parade they made! A long line of dancing children formed behind the pied piper.

Soon all the children in town were following the pied piper as he led them toward the river. All of the parents suddenly became very afraid.

Would their children jump in the river as the rats had done? Just then, the pied piper made a turn.

Soon the pied piper and the long line of dancing children reached the base of the mountain near the town. The townspeople were amazed as a magic door suddenly opened in the mountainside.

The pied piper led all the children toward the door. The poor people of Hamelin cried as they watched the pied piper lead their children through the magic door, never to be seen again.

The children of Hamelin went to live beyond the mountain in a land that was always filled with happiness and laughter and sunshine. And there definitely were no rats!

The Twelve Dancing Princesses

From the adaptation by Sarah Toast
Illustrated by Pamela R. Levy

Long ago there lived a king and his twelve beautiful daughters. The princesses all slept in one huge bedroom. Even though the king carefully locked their door each night, the princesses were tired and out of sorts every morning. More puzzling still, their silk slippers were worn to shreds.

Determined to find out the truth, the king issued a proclamation declaring that whoever could solve the mystery of where the twelve princesses went to dance every night could choose a wife from among them. If, however, the suitor failed to discover the secret within three days and nights, he would be banished from the kingdom forever.

Then one day a poor soldier came limping along the road. He had heard about the proclamation, and he wanted to try to marry a princess, too. He had stopped to rest and eat when an old beggar woman shuffled by.

He did not have much food, but he offered to share with the woman nevertheless.

"You have shown me great kindness," said the woman. "To repay you, I will tell you this: do not drink the wine the princesses offer you. Pretend to fall asleep. And take this cloak, which will make you invisible. Follow the princesses to learn their secret!"

The soldier arrived at the castle that evening and was led to the little room next to the princesses'. Soon the eldest princess brought the soldier a cup of wine. He pretended to drink it, letting it trickle down under his chin onto his scarf. Then he pretended to fall asleep.

Soon the twelve princesses put on their new silk slippers. Then the eldest princess tapped on her bedpost three times. The bed descended into the floor and became a flight of stairs. The soldier threw on the cloak and followed them down the stairway.

Eventually they came to a forest of gold, silver, and diamond trees. As the princesses hurried through, the soldier reached up and broke off a branch from each so he would have a way to prove his story.

At the edge of a lake, twelve princes in boats awaited the princesses. The princes rowed them across the lake to a castle, where the princesses danced the night away. The invisible soldier sneaked into a boat and went too.

Hours later they hurried back the way they had come. The soldier was able to dash ahead, throw off his cloak, and jump into bed. The princesses never knew they had been followed.

The next morning the king sent for the soldier and asked him, "Have you discovered where my daughters dance their shoes to shreds every night?"

"Your Highness, I have," said the soldier. "They go down a hidden staircase. Then they walk through an enchanted forest to a beautiful lake. Twelve princes take them across the lake to a castle where they dance all night."

The king couldn't believe the soldier's story until the soldier showed him the branches of silver, gold, and diamonds. Then the king summoned his daughters, who at last admitted the truth.

The king told the soldier that he could choose one of the princesses to be his wife.

The soldier was given royal chambers and royal garments to wear. He and the eldest princess were married, and the wedding guests happily danced the night away.

Patch's Lucky Star

Adapted by Brian Conway
Illustrated by Loretta Lustig

Patch was a pretty little turtle who lived by the pond. She was as quiet and careful as a turtle could be. Most turtles her age romped along the shores of the pond all day, but Patch did not.

Patch looked just like any other young turtle she knew, except for one thing. She had a yellow patch on the outside of her shell. Patch was the only turtle at the pond to have such a shell. "It is such an odd shell for a turtle to have," Patch thought to herself.

"It's not odd," Patch's mother would tell her. "It's just different. It makes you special."

Patch did not want to be special. She just wanted a normal shell so everyone would stop looking at her patch.

Patch would hide away most of the day in the tall grass. She would go to her favorite spots on the pond only when she knew no one was around.

Most days, Patch just tucked herself up inside her shell and stayed there. Patch liked staying inside her shell very much. It was dark and quiet, and Patch could be all alone.

Most of all, though, Patch did not want to have to look at her own shell. She thought the big yellow patch was terrible. In fact, she thought it made her whole shell look terrible. So Patch stayed inside her shell.

One day, Diamond and Snapper walked by Patch's hiding place. They came up and tapped on her shell.

"Patch!" they called. "Come exploring with us." But Patch just stayed very still in her shell. Soon, Diamond and Snapper went away.

Later that day, Patch heard her mother's voice outside her shell. Poking her head out, Patch was surprised to see Diamond and Snapper's mother there, too.

"Have you seen Diamond or Snapper?" Patch's mother asked. "They've been gone for several hours."

"They went exploring," Patch told her mother.

Diamond and Snapper's mother shook her head. "We'll have to go looking for those two," she said. "It is getting dark."

"You stay here, Patch," her mother said. "We do not need another lost turtle."

Patch shivered, glad she had stayed inside her shell. She thought it must be scary to be lost on the pond at night. Then she saw that the stars were starting to glitter in the sky.

"If only my shell could shine as brightly as the stars," she thought aloud. "Then I wouldn't mind my patch so much."

As Patch sighed, she heard Diamond and Snapper calling for their mother. Their mother called back to them. Their voices were coming closer to Patch's place on the shore.

Patch quickly ducked back into her shell. Soon it seemed that all the turtles were just outside, huddled around her.

Everyone was talking all at once. "We kept going in circles," said Snapper.

"Everything looked the same in the dark," said Diamond. "But then we saw Patch's bright yellow patch all the way across the pond."

"We followed Patch's patch all the way back!" said Snapper.

"If you ever get lost again," said Diamond and Snapper's mother, "be sure to follow the bright North Star."

"We don't need the North Star," Diamond and Snapper said. "We've got our own star right here on the shore, and it's the brightest star on the pond, that's for sure!"

"Patch, they're talking about your special shell!" said Patch's mother.

Patch had never been so happy. She popped her head out so she could look back at her patch. In the moonlight, it shined very brightly.

From that day on, Patch loved to look at her shell. She hoped her star would shine all the time. It was a very special patch indeed.

Sleeping Beauty

From the adaptation by Brian Conway
Illustrated by Holly Jones

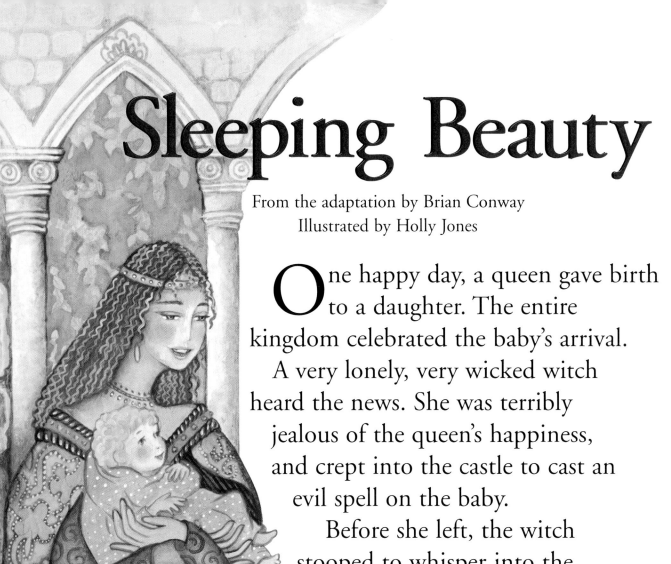

One happy day, a queen gave birth to a daughter. The entire kingdom celebrated the baby's arrival. A very lonely, very wicked witch heard the news. She was terribly jealous of the queen's happiness, and crept into the castle to cast an evil spell on the baby.

Before she left, the witch stooped to whisper into the baby's ear. "When you reach the age of sixteen, you will have a simple sewing accident.

"You will prick your finger and fall into a deep sleep… and never awaken!" cackled the witch.

Years later, the princess's sixteenth birthday arrived. As the princess put on a dress for her party, she noticed it was torn. She found a needle and thread and began to mend the dress. As she stitched, the princess pricked her finger. She fell to the floor in a deep sleep.

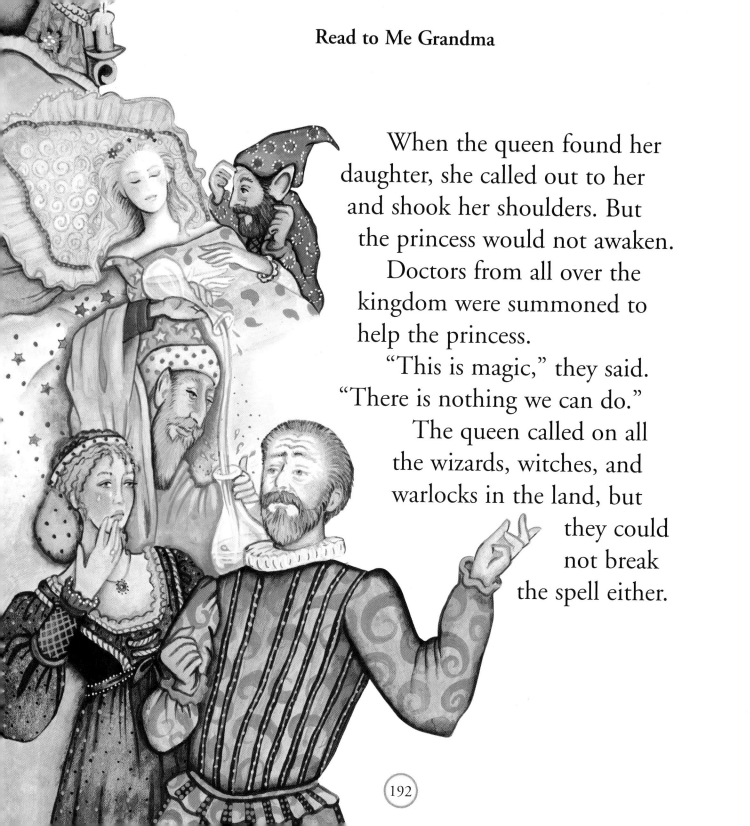

When the queen found her daughter, she called out to her and shook her shoulders. But the princess would not awaken. Doctors from all over the kingdom were summoned to help the princess.

"This is magic," they said. "There is nothing we can do."

The queen called on all the wizards, witches, and warlocks in the land, but they could not break the spell either.

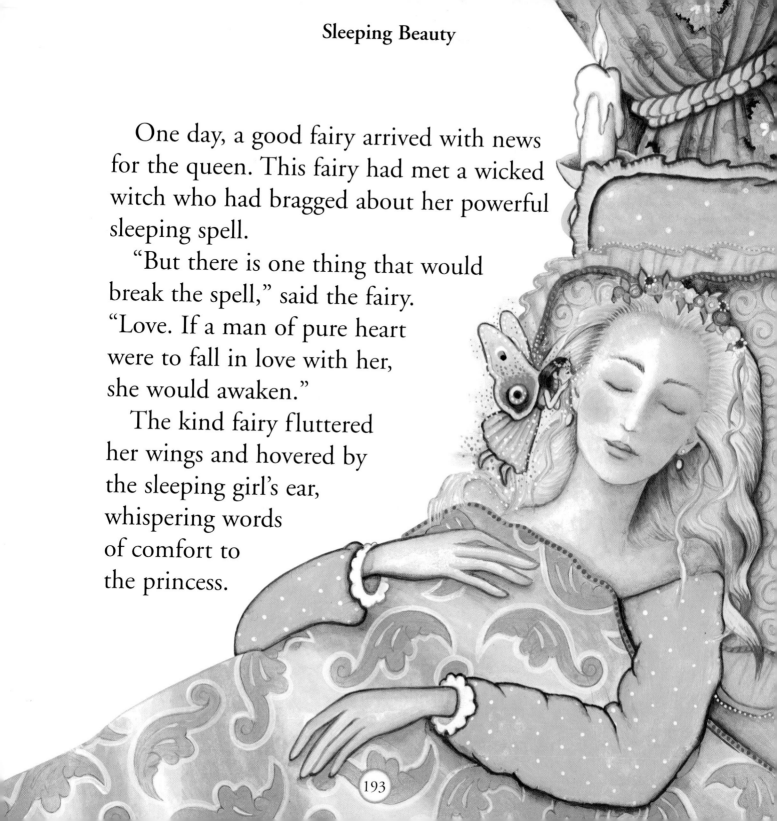

One day, a good fairy arrived with news for the queen. This fairy had met a wicked witch who had bragged about her powerful sleeping spell.

"But there is one thing that would break the spell," said the fairy. "Love. If a man of pure heart were to fall in love with her, she would awaken."

The kind fairy fluttered her wings and hovered by the sleeping girl's ear, whispering words of comfort to the princess.

"What man could fall in love with a sleeping girl?" sobbed the queen. "All hope is surely lost!"

"I cannot awaken your daughter," said the fairy, "but I can make you, and everyone in your castle, fall asleep until the day she wakes. Then you will not have to wait in sorrow."

The queen agreed. The fairy cast her spell, and all the people in the castle fell into a deep sleep.

One hundred years passed. A dense, dark forest grew around the silent castle.

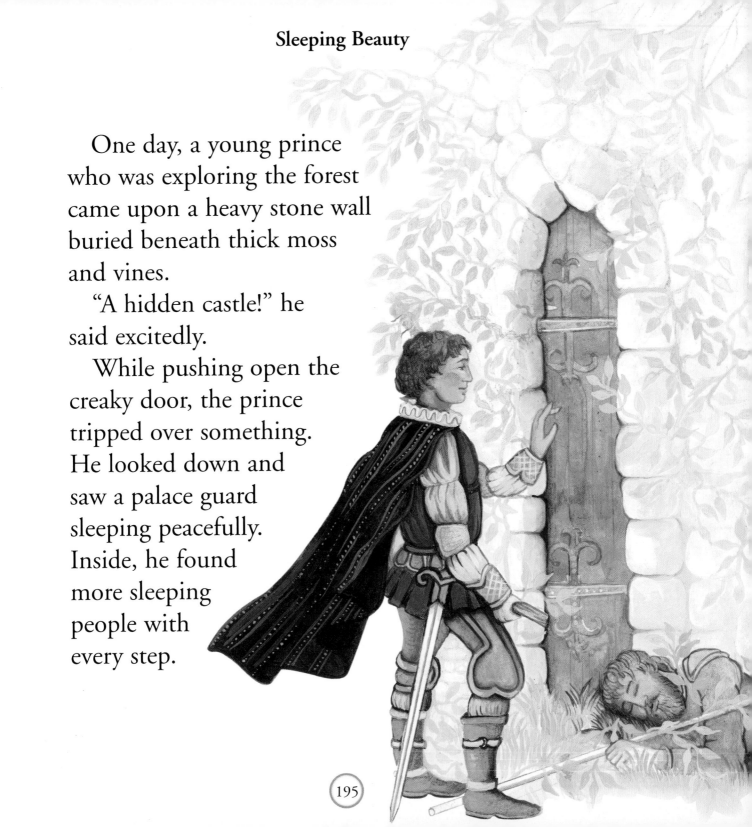

One day, a young prince who was exploring the forest came upon a heavy stone wall buried beneath thick moss and vines.

"A hidden castle!" he said excitedly.

While pushing open the creaky door, the prince tripped over something. He looked down and saw a palace guard sleeping peacefully. Inside, he found more sleeping people with every step.

Soon the prince came to the room where the princess lay in her deep sleep.

"A sleeping beauty," he whispered in awe. Overcome with emotion, the prince lifted her soft white hand and gently kissed it.

At that kiss, the princess's eyes opened in a flash.

"You have come to me at last!" she said. "I was waiting for you in my dream. A kind fairy told me you would come!"

At the same moment the princess awakened, so too did the queen and her sleeping subjects.

"The princess is awake at last!" they cheered.

"This prince has saved us," said the princess, with love and gratitude shining in her eyes.

In a few short days, the prince and princess were married. The princess had truly found the man of her dreams, and they lived happily ever after.

The Little Dutch Boy

Adapted by Sarah Toast
Illustrated by Linda Dockey Graves

Long ago there was a boy named Hans who lived with his mother in a pretty town in Holland. The land of Holland is very flat, and much of it is below the level of the sea. The farmers in Holland built big walls called dikes to keep the sea from flooding their land.

One day Hans' mother packed a basket of bread and cheese for Hans to take to their old friend Mr. Van Notten.

Mr. Van Notten lived outside of town, and it was a long way to his house. Mr. Van Notten had only an old dog to keep him company, so he was very happy when Hans came to visit him. To get to Mr. Van Notten's home, Hans just followed the main road out of town. This road ran right alongside a dike.

Hans was very hungry after his long walk, so Mr. Van Notten set out the bread and cheese from the basket and made some cocoa.

After their meal, Hans noticed that the sky had become dark and stormy. He decided that he should leave right away to get home before it started to rain.

Hans walked quickly, but it was not long before cold, stinging raindrops battered him as he struggled against the powerful wind. Hans had no idea he was nearing the town until he saw the dike. It meant he would soon be home.

Hans noticed a small hole in the dike and a trickle of water seeping through the stones. He knew the storm must have whipped up the waves of the sea, and the water had made a crack in the dike.

The Little Dutch Boy

"The dike is breaking!" Hans shouted, but no one heard him. All the windows in the houses had been shuttered because of the storm.

Hans knew that if the hole in the dike got big enough, the sea would surely push its way through and all would be lost. The sea would flood the farms and wash away the little town.

Hans quickly came up with a plan. He balled up his fist and pushed it into the hole. Suddenly, the steady stream of water stopped! Hans was very proud and happy that one small boy could hold back the sea.

Hans was sure his worried mother would soon send people to look for him. But minutes turned into hours.

As darkness fell, Hans became very cold and tired, and his arm began to ache. He had to force himself to keep standing on his tired legs. To keep himself going, Hans thought about how important it was to hold back the water of the sea.

As Hans stood in the cold rain by the dike, he thought about the warmth of the fireplace at home. Then he thought about how good it was going to feel to lie down in his snug bed. These thoughts helped the exhausted boy get through the long, cold night.

When Hans did not come home that evening, his mother began to worry. Even while the rain was falling, she kept looking out the door for Hans to come back. At last she decided that Hans must have waited out the storm at Mr. Van Notten's house. She thought he must have spent the night there because it was too dark to come home after the storm.

After looking out the door one more time, Hans's mother closed up the house and went to bed.

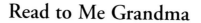

But Hans' mother could not sleep. She was too worried about her son.

Early the next morning, Mr. Van Notten decided to take a walk to Hans' home. He wanted to thank Hans' mother for the tasty food.

Soon Mr. Van Notten came upon Hans. The boy was cold and trembling, and his arm hurt from keeping his fist in the hole in the dike all night.

Mr. Van Notten could not believe his eyes! He told Hans to hold firm for just a little while longer. Then Mr. Van Notten ran toward the town to get help.

The Little Dutch Boy

Soon Mr. Van Notten returned with someone to take care of Hans and some materials to repair the dike. Hans was wrapped in blankets and carried home. His mother was so happy to see him!

She put Hans in his bed and gave him warm broth to eat, and the town doctor came by to check on him. Hans was all right, but he was so tired that he fell asleep right away and did not wake up until the following day.

Everyone in town came to thank Hans for holding back the mighty sea. The mayor presented Hans with a medal, and all the people cheered! Hans would forever be remembered as a hero.

George and the Dragon

From the adaptation by Brian Conway
Illustrated by Tammie Speer Lyon

Once upon a time, there lived a boy named George. The queen of fairies had taken him in as a baby, and the fairies raised him as their own. They taught him to be a brave and noble knight.

At last the time came when George was old enough to seek out his destiny. The queen of fairies called him to see her.

"Your journey starts today," she told him. "You have many adventures before you now."

"Yes, Your Majesty." George bowed before the queen. He was sad to leave the land of the fairies, but he was not afraid.

George and the Dragon

In his travels, George heard countless stories of the hardship that had befallen the kingdom of Silene. George decided that was where he was needed most, and headed on his way.

When George reached Silene, he found that a high wall enclosed the castle and the small city around it. He saw no one at all, except for a young lady who had rushed out to meet him.

"You would do well to leave here now and never return," said the lady.

"But I have come to help you," George replied, "even if it costs me my life."

"Very well. I am Princess Sabra," she said. The princess told George why the kingdom lived in fear. A dragon had slain their king, and now kept the villagers captive inside the city walls. The dragon demanded that he be given two sheep to eat each day, or he would eat the people themselves for his dinner!

"We gave up our last two sheep this morning," continued the princess. "Tomorrow we shall have nothing to give the dragon, and we shall all perish. What's more," she went on, "the dragon cannot be killed by sword alone; his scales are tougher than steel. Many have already died trying to defeat him."

Suddenly George remembered a gift the fairy queen had given him. It was an hourglass, filled with tiny blue grains of sand that looked as cold as ice. The hourglass bore an inscription which read: *There is one way to save the rest: the Serpent's weakness is in his breath.*

George and Sabra hurried to the dragon's lair. "The time left in the hourglass will lead us," George whispered. "We must wait until all the sand has dropped through, then we should know what to do."

"We *should* know?" Sabra asked. "And what shall happen if we don't?"

George and Sabra arrived at the dragon's lair just as the dragon awoke from a deep slumber. As the dragon stretched and yawned a great, fiery yawn, the very last tiny blue grain of sand was dropping through the hourglass.

George knew what must be done. He threw the hourglass at the dragon's yawning mouth. It shattered on the dragon's tongue in a cloud of icy mist.

The magical hourglass, which had actually contained crystals of frozen time, instantly froze shut the dragon's mouth! He had to live the rest of his days deep beneath the warm waters of a nearby lake, so that he would not freeze from the inside out.

George had saved the kingdom. In her gratitude, Sabra offered George all the riches she possessed. But George wanted no payment for his deeds. "I have many more adventures left to face," George told Sabra. "They are my greatest reward."

The Little Mermaid

From the adaptation by Lynne Suesse
Illustrated by Pamela R. Levy

Deep below the ocean waves, there was once a kingdom of mermaids and mermen. Here there lived a family with six beautiful daughters. Each daughter looked forward to her eighteenth birthday, when she would be allowed to swim to the surface for her first look at the sky.

When it was the littlest mermaid's eighteenth birthday, she rushed up to peek above the waves. It was even more beautiful than she had imagined!

Soon she spied a ship, and spent
nearly an hour watching the humans.
One of them was particularly
handsome. The little mermaid
realized he must be a prince.

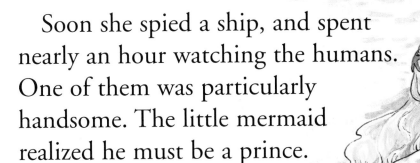

Suddenly, a terrible
storm began. The
prince's ship was
torn to pieces by the
pounding waves.

The little mermaid knew
the prince could not live in the
water, and took him safely to shore.
The little mermaid brushed the
hair from the prince's face and
looked into his eyes, but became
frightened and quickly swam away.

Back under the ocean, the little mermaid
told her sisters about the handsome prince. As
she told her story, she realized that she
could not live without him.

That night, the little mermaid snuck away
to see the sea witch. She knew the sea witch
could give her what she wanted most.

The sea witch told the little mermaid
that she would be happy to give her the
legs she longed for, but there was a
price for such a special gift: her
voice. She would be able to
walk and dance, but unable
to speak or sing.

216

The little mermaid agreed to the sea
witch's demand, and swam to the surface
to drink the magic potion. For a moment,
she felt very strange. When she looked down,
she saw that her tail had become two beautiful
human legs!

On his morning walk, the prince discovered the
beautiful girl on the beach. He asked her who she
was and where she came from, but she could make
no sound. The prince wrapped his cloak around the
little mermaid, and took her back to the castle.

The prince was enchanted by this lovely girl. He felt that he had met her somewhere before. The two spent every moment together, taking long walks and gazing into each other's eyes. Even though the princess never uttered a word, the prince fell deeply in love.

Finally one day the prince announced to his parents, the king and queen, that he planned to marry this beautiful, silent girl. The king and queen forbade it! They wanted the prince to marry a princess, not a mysterious stranger. But when they saw the light of true love shining in their son's eyes, they gave their consent.

218

On the happiest day of the little mermaid's life, she and the handsome prince were married.

The best part of all was that the power of the prince's love overcame the evil in the sea witch's spell! The little mermaid kept her legs, and the moment they were married, she also regained her voice.

The first words spoken by the new princess were "I do."

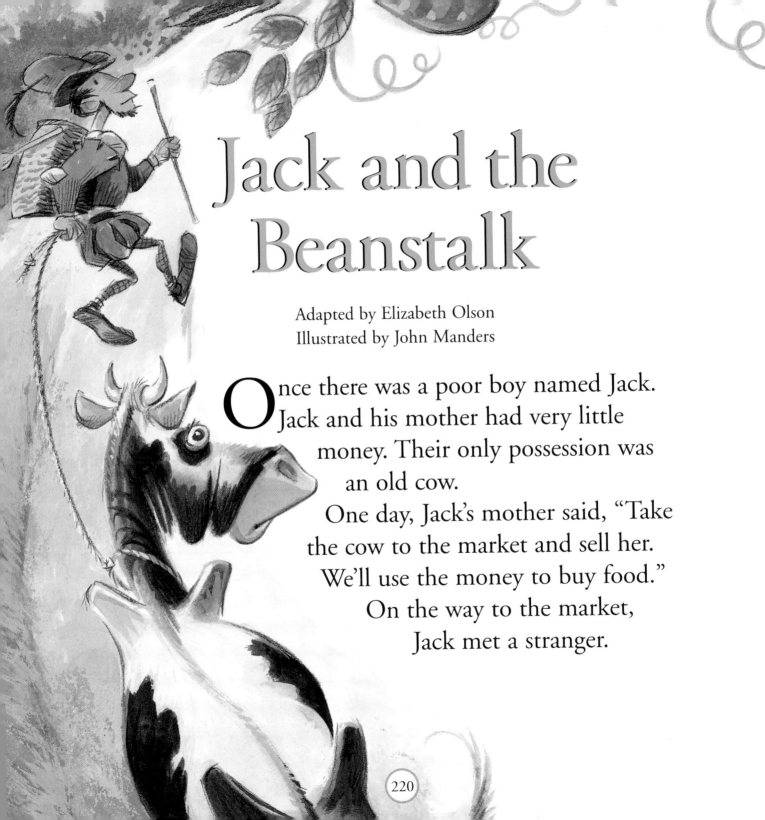

Jack and the Beanstalk

Adapted by Elizabeth Olson
Illustrated by John Manders

Once there was a poor boy named Jack. Jack and his mother had very little money. Their only possession was an old cow.

One day, Jack's mother said, "Take the cow to the market and sell her. We'll use the money to buy food."

On the way to the market, Jack met a stranger.

"I'll give you five magic beans for that old cow," offered the stranger.

Jack accepted the deal at once, and ran straight home to tell his mother the news.

"What have you done?" she shouted. "We can't buy food with magic beans."

She threw the beans out the window, and sent Jack to bed.

The next morning, Jack awoke to find that a beanstalk had grown from the magic beans! It reached all the way to the clouds.

221

Jack and the Beanstalk

Jack climbed up the beanstalk until he found himself above the clouds. To Jack's surprise, he saw a huge castle.

As he got closer, Jack realized the castle must be the home of a giant. The doors were so big, Jack could walk beneath them.

Once inside, Jack wandered into a room where a giant was counting gold coins. Suddenly the giant looked up and bellowed, "Fee-fi-fo-fum! I smell the blood of an Englishman!" The giant looked around, but didn't see tiny Jack. After a while, the giant left the room.

Jack saw his chance. He snatched a gold coin and ran from the castle. He finally reached the beanstalk, threw the coin down into his mother's garden, and climbed down as fast as he could.

With the gold coin, Jack and his mother bought food and made their house comfortable. But one day the money ran out. Jack knew that he had to return to the castle.

He climbed back up the beanstalk. This time he found the giant holding a hen. "Lay!" yelled the giant, and the hen laid a golden egg. When the giant walked away with the egg, leaving the hen behind, Jack grabbed the hen and took it to his mother.

Curious about the giant's treasures, Jack climbed the beanstalk one more time. He found the giant with a tiny harp. "Play!" yelled the giant, and the harp sang a beautiful song. Within minutes, the giant had fallen asleep.

Jack tiptoed over to the harp. Suddenly, in a loud, clear voice, the harp sang out, "Someone is stealing me!"

225

The giant woke up immediately. "Fee-fi-fo-fum! I see the face of an Englishman!" Jack grabbed the harp and dashed out of the castle. He ran through the clouds to the beanstalk. The harp sang for her life all the while.

"Sssshh! I am rescuing you from the giant," said Jack. Finally, the harp understood. She began to sing a happy song.

With the giant close behind, Jack climbed down the beanstalk. He gave the harp to his mother and picked up an ax. With three mighty swings Jack chopped down the beanstalk. Jack and his mother never saw the giant again.

With the golden eggs from the hen and the sweet music of the harp, Jack and his mother lived happily ever after.

Snow White

Adapted by Jane Jerrard
Illustrated by Barbara Lanza

Long ago in a far-off land, a princess was born with skin so pale and lovely that she was called Snow White. As the baby grew into a young girl, she became more and more beautiful each year.

Her stepmother, the queen, was also very beautiful. The queen had a magical mirror, and every day she would look into it and ask, "Mirror, mirror, on the wall, who is the fairest of us all?" The mirror always would answer, "You, my queen, are the fairest in the land." And the queen would be very pleased because she knew that it was true.

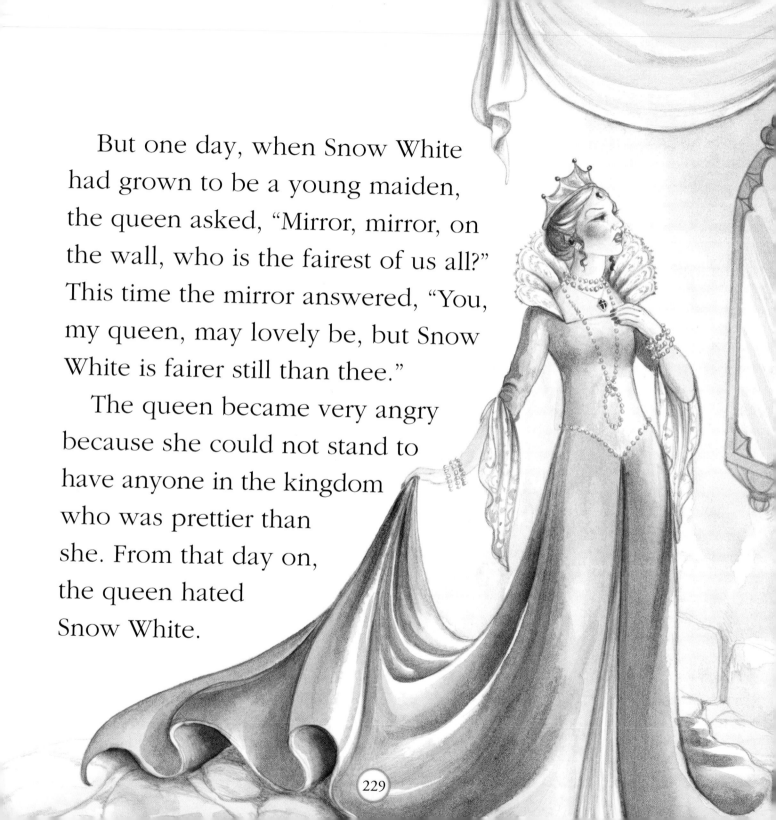

But one day, when Snow White had grown to be a young maiden, the queen asked, "Mirror, mirror, on the wall, who is the fairest of us all?" This time the mirror answered, "You, my queen, may lovely be, but Snow White is fairer still than thee."

The queen became very angry because she could not stand to have anyone in the kingdom who was prettier than she. From that day on, the queen hated Snow White.

When the queen could no longer bear to look at the beautiful princess, she called a woodsman and ordered him to take Snow White away from the castle forever. The woodsman took Snow White deep into the dark forest and left her there all alone.

Snow White became very afraid. She heard mysterious noises and saw frightening shadows. Snow White was so scared that she began to run as fast and as far as she could. Finally, she came upon a little cottage.

When no one answered her knocks, Snow White went inside. There she found a little table set with seven plates, and seven little beds were lined up against the wall. The hungry princess nibbled a bit of food from each plate, then she threw herself down on the seventh bed and fell asleep.

Seven dwarfs shared this little cottage. Soon they came back from the gold mine where they worked.

How surprised the dwarfs were to find Snow White
sleeping in their home! They let the lovely girl sleep
until morning, and then they asked her how she found
her way to their cottage deep in the woods. When
they heard Snow White's story, they felt sorry for her
and asked her to stay.

Snow White took care of the cottage, and the dwarfs gave her food, friendship, and shelter in return. Snow White was happy living with the dwarfs.

But one day back at the castle, the evil queen again asked, "Mirror, mirror, on the wall, who is the fairest of us all?" The mirror replied, "You, my queen, may lovely be, but Snow White is fairer still than thee."

The queen then knew that Snow White was still alive, so she quickly made a plan to get rid of Snow White by herself. The queen soon found out where Snow White was staying, and she went to the dwarfs' cottage disguised as an old woman.

When Snow White saw the old woman at the door, she invited her in. Snow White did not know that the old woman was really the queen. The queen offered Snow White an apple, and when Snow White took a bite, she instantly fell to the floor. The queen had placed poison inside the apple!

With a shriek of laughter, the queen rushed back to the castle. She hurried up the steps and ran to her mirror. Once again the queen asked, "Mirror, mirror, on the wall, who is the fairest of us all?"

This time the mirror replied, "Gone is the beauty of Snow White, and you are the fairest in my sight."

Soon the dwarfs finished their daily work and came back to their cottage. They found Snow White on the floor, but they could not wake her. The dwarfs decided to lay her in a glass case so they could watch over her.

One day a prince came by and saw Snow White lying in the case. She was the most beautiful princess he had ever seen, and he fell in love with her instantly. The prince opened the glass case and lifted Snow White into his arms. As soon as he did this, a piece of the poison apple fell from Snow White's mouth, and she awoke from her deep sleep.

Snow White

Snow White slowly opened her eyes and looked up at the prince's face. She saw that his eyes were filled with love. At that moment, she too fell in love.

The next day, the queen once again asked her mirror who was the fairest in the land. The mirror answered, "You, my queen, may lovely be, but the bride, Snow White, is fairer still than thee." The queen could only shriek in anger, knowing that she had failed to get rid of Snow White.

That same day the dwarfs danced with joy as Snow White and the prince were married right there in the dwarfs' garden.

The Flying Prince

From the adaptation by Brian Conway
Illustrated by Kathi Ember

Prince Rashar lived in a distant land. He spent each day hunting and exploring the jungle. While hunting, Prince Rashar saw a large parrot land on a branch above him.

"I am the king of the parrots," it said proudly.

"How is it that you can talk?" asked the prince.

"Princess Saledra gave me that power," he said.

"Interesting… Where can I find this princess?" Prince Rashar asked.

"You could never find her," squawked the Parrot King. "She lives far away, in the city where night becomes day."

Curious, Prince Rashar decided to find Princess Saledra, and rode off into the jungle.

Soon, Prince Rashar came upon four trolls having an argument.

"Excuse me," the prince said. "Perhaps I can help."

"Our master left us these four magic things," the trolls answered. "But he did not tell us which of us gets what!"

There was a flying carpet that would take its owner wherever he wished to go. There was a cloth bag that would give its holder anything he wished for. And there was a magic bowl and a magic stick.

"I can help you decide fairly," said the clever prince. "I will shoot an arrow into the jungle. Whoever returns with the arrow shall keep all of the magic items."

Prince Rashar shot an arrow into the air, and the trolls dashed into the jungle to find it. While they searched, Prince Rashar took the magic items. He rolled out the carpet and sat down on it.

"Carpet, take me to the city where night becomes day," he said.

The magic carpet zoomed through the air, stopping at last in a faraway city. As night began to fall, the prince went to the palace to call on the princess. When the sun set, the city was dark for a moment. Then a door opened at the roof of the palace. Princess Saledra walked out from her room and stepped across the palace rooftop.

Her beauty shone more brightly than the moon. In an instant, night became day. Prince Rashar could not take his eyes off her.

At that moment, he knew he loved the princess.

Prince Rashar took his bag of wishes and said, "Bag, give me a gift that the princess will love." He reached into the bag and found an exquisite silk shawl that matched the princess's gown exactly.

241

Later that night, after the princess had gone inside, Prince Rashar asked his magic carpet to take him to the room where Princess Saledra slept. The carpet lifted the prince to the palace roof, and he crept through the door to the princess's room.

Princess Saledra was sleeping soundly in her bed. The prince set the shawl beside her. He stopped to gaze upon her beautiful face.

Just then, the princess awoke! She was frightened at first, but the prince explained who he was. The princess saw that he was a very handsome man and that he spoke from his heart. Her heart softened further when she saw his gift to her. The princess smiled the brightest smile ever seen.

At that moment, Prince Rashar and Princess Saledra fell in love. They were soon married. And each day forever after, the prince and princess flew over their kingdom on the magic carpet.

Rumpelstiltskin

From the adaptation by Anne H. Foley
Illustrated by David Hohn

A miller and his daughter once delivered some flour to the king. To impress the king, the miller boasted, "Your Majesty, my daughter is very special. She can spin ordinary straw into gold!"

"Indeed!" said the greedy king. "She must prove her talent."

The king led the girl to a room filled with straw. "Spin all of this into gold by tomorrow morning," he said, shutting the door.

244

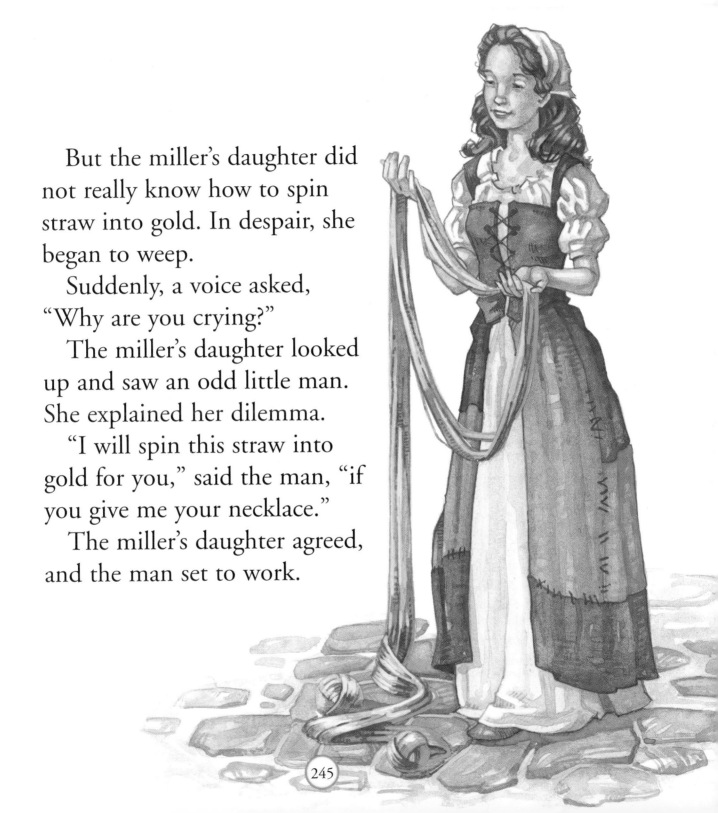

But the miller's daughter did not really know how to spin straw into gold. In despair, she began to weep.

Suddenly, a voice asked, "Why are you crying?"

The miller's daughter looked up and saw an odd little man. She explained her dilemma.

"I will spin this straw into gold for you," said the man, "if you give me your necklace."

The miller's daughter agreed, and the man set to work.

The next morning, the king was delighted to see that all the straw had been spun into gold. He led the miller's daughter to another, much larger room filled with straw.

"Spin all of this into gold by tomorrow morning, and you shall become queen," said the king, leaving the room.

"I cannot do it!" she sobbed. Just then the little man reappeared. "I will do it for you," he said, "if you give me your firstborn child."

The miller's daughter felt she had no choice, and agreed to the awful request. She slept as the little man worked.

By sunrise, all of the straw had once again been turned to gold.

"You are a woman of incredible skill, and I would like you to be my wife!" cried the king upon seeing the miracle.

The miller's daughter and the king were soon married.

Within a year, the queen gave birth to a daughter. She forgot all about her agreement with the little man, until one day when he suddenly appeared. "I have not forgotten our deal," he said. "Give me your daughter."

"Oh please, do not take my child!" pleaded the desperate queen.

"Very well; I will give you another chance," he said.

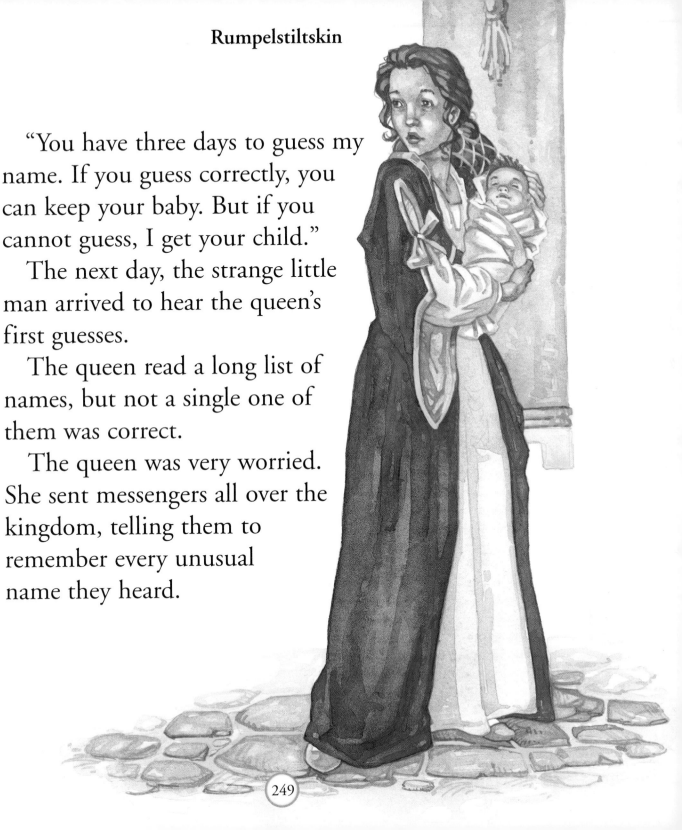

"You have three days to guess my name. If you guess correctly, you can keep your baby. But if you cannot guess, I get your child."

The next day, the strange little man arrived to hear the queen's first guesses.

The queen read a long list of names, but not a single one of them was correct.

The queen was very worried. She sent messengers all over the kingdom, telling them to remember every unusual name they heard.

When the little man returned, the queen read a list of all the odd names found by her messengers. But at the end of the second day, she still did not know his name. On the third day, a messenger came running into the palace.

"Your Majesty, I have seen an odd little man dancing around a fire, singing:

The queen's heart will break,
For her child I'll take.
I'll win the guessing game,
For Rumpelstiltskin is my name!"

Soon the little man arrived.
The queen looked him in the
eye and asked, "Is your name
Rumpelstiltskin?"

"How did you know?" screamed
the little man, stomping his feet in
anger. He stomped so hard that he
kicked a hole right through the
floor! In an instant, the
strange little man
disappeared, never
to be seen again.

The Three Billy Goats Gruff

Adapted by Carolyn Quattrocki
Illustrated by Tim Ellis

Once there were three Billy Goats Gruff. The oldest was Big Billy Goat Gruff, who wore a collar of thick black braid. Middle Billy Goat Gruff had a red collar around his neck, and Little Billy Goat Gruff wore a yellow one.

Big Billy Goat Gruff had a deep billy goat voice. Middle Billy Goat Gruff had a middle-size billy goat voice. And Little Billy Goat Gruff had a very high billy goat voice. All winter long the three of them lived on a rocky hillside.

Every day during the cold winter months the three Billy Goats Gruff played among the rocks. Little Billy Goat Gruff would call out in his little billy goat voice, "Watch this!" as he leaped over little rocks. Middle Billy Goat Gruff would shout, "Watch this!" as he leaped over middle-size rocks. Big Billy Goat Gruff would bellow in his big billy goat voice, "WATCH THIS!" as he leaped over great big rocks.

One night a strong, cold wind was blowing. Big Billy Goat Gruff said, "It is time for us to find a warm place to stay." So the three Billy Goats Gruff found a nice, cozy cave to sleep in. During the cold nights they dreamed of springtime.

When spring finally arrived, the three Billy Goats Gruff looked longingly across the rushing river. "How I would love to go up the mountains on the other side of the river," said Little Billy Goat Gruff.

"The grass is green, and the flowers are pretty. There is plenty to eat on that side."

"To get to the mountains," said Middle Billy Goat Gruff, "we will have to cross the bridge over the river." The three Billy Goats Gruff knew that a mean, ugly troll lived under the bridge. The troll had eyes that were as big as saucers, a head of shaggy hair, and a nose that was as long as a flute.

One day Big Billy Goat Gruff thought of a plan to trick the troll so they could cross the bridge. The next morning the three Billy Goats Gruff went down to the river. Little Billy Goat Gruff started to cross the bridge. *Trip-trap, trip-trap, trip-trap* went Little Billy Goat Gruff's feet on the wooden bridge.

"Who's that *trip-trapping* across my bridge?" roared the troll.

"It is only I, Little Billy Goat Gruff," said the little billy goat.

"I'm coming to eat you up!" hollered the troll.

"Oh no!" cried Little Billy Goat Gruff. "I am only a tiny, little billy goat. Wait for my brother, Middle Billy Goat Gruff. He will make a much bigger dinner for you to eat." So the troll let the little goat go across.

When Middle Billy Goat Gruff started to cross the bridge, the troll hollered, "I'm coming to eat you up!"

"Oh no!" cried Middle Billy Goat Gruff. "I am only a middle-size billy goat. Wait for my brother, Big Billy Goat Gruff. He will make a much bigger dinner for you to eat." So the troll let Middle Billy Goat Gruff cross the bridge to the other side.

Finally, Big Billy Goat Gruff came to the bridge.

TRIP-TRAP, *TRIP-TRAP*, *TRIP-TRAP* went Big Billy Goat Gruff's feet as he walked across the bridge.

"Who's that *TRIP-TRAPPING* across my bridge?" roared the troll.

"It is I, Big Billy Goat Gruff," said the billy goat.

"I'm coming to eat you up!" hollered the troll.

"Come ahead!" said Big Billy Goat Gruff. So the troll climbed up onto the bridge and came toward Big Billy Goat Gruff.

Suddenly, Little Billy Goat Gruff and Middle Billy Goat Gruff called out from the other side of the bridge. "Look out, troll!" they hollered.

The troll quickly turned toward the smaller billy goats. Suddenly, Big Billy Goat Gruff, with his two big horns, tossed the troll high into the air!

The troll fell swiftly down into the river below with a huge splash.

Big Billy Goat Gruff happily joined Little Billy Goat Gruff and Middle Billy Goat Gruff on the other side of the bridge. There they feasted on the green grass and the wildflowers. From then on, they could cross the wooden bridge whenever they pleased.

The Princess and the Pea

Adapted by Lora Kalkman
Illustrated by Carolyn Croll

A handsome prince lived in a faraway land with his parents, the king and queen. More than anything, the prince wanted to get married and have a family of his own.

So he set out to find a special princess to be his bride, traveling to kingdoms far and wide. The prince met many beautiful princesses, all of whom wanted to marry him.

But the prince did not think any of the princesses were special enough.

After his long search, the prince gave up and returned to the castle. The king and queen saw how downhearted their son was and decided to help. They planned a royal ball, inviting all the princesses in the kingdom. All of the princesses wanted to marry the prince. But the prince found something wrong with every one of them.

Three days later a princess from a distant kingdom was traveling near the prince's castle, when suddenly it began to rain. Thunder crashed, and lightning flashed. The storm scared the horses, and the carriage got stuck in the mud.

"What shall we do?" asked the princess's driver. "The horses cannot move the carriage another inch."

The princess was very smart. "I will walk to that castle nearby and ask if we can spend the night," she said. "Surely they will help us."

Wet from the rain and covered in mud, the princess knocked on the heavy door of the castle. When the prince opened the door, he was stunned at the sight of the girl. The princess explained her plight, and the prince invited her to stay.

The queen asked the servants to fix up a special bed just for the girl. The servants stacked up twenty comfy mattresses and twenty fluffy quilts. Then the queen tucked a tiny green pea underneath the bottom mattress.

"If she is truly a princess," said the queen, "she will not be able to sleep. Only a true princess will be able to feel the hard pea under all these layers."

Exhausted from her journey, the princess climbed a ladder and got into the tall, cozy bed.

But when the princess snuggled in, she did not feel comfortable at all.

This tall bed is awfully lumpy and bumpy, she thought. *It feels like there is a giant rock in the bed!*

Although the princess was very tired, she was not able to sleep. She tossed and turned all night long in the lumpy, bumpy bed.

The next morning, the princess walked to the royal garden to meet the king, queen, and prince for breakfast.

"How did you sleep?" asked the queen.

"Not very well," admitted the princess. "In fact, I couldn't sleep a wink! I found this pea underneath the bottom mattress of my bed." The princess held out the tiny pea for the queen to see.

The queen was delighted. *Only a real princess would feel the pea,* she thought.

Only a special princess could feel the pea, the prince thought happily. Surely, this was the special princess he had been looking for! The prince asked the princess to marry him. The king and queen planned a joyful wedding and invited everyone in the kingdom. The prince and princess got married, and everyone lived happily ever after.

Pinocchio

From the adaptation by Elizabeth Olson
Illustrated by David Austin Clar

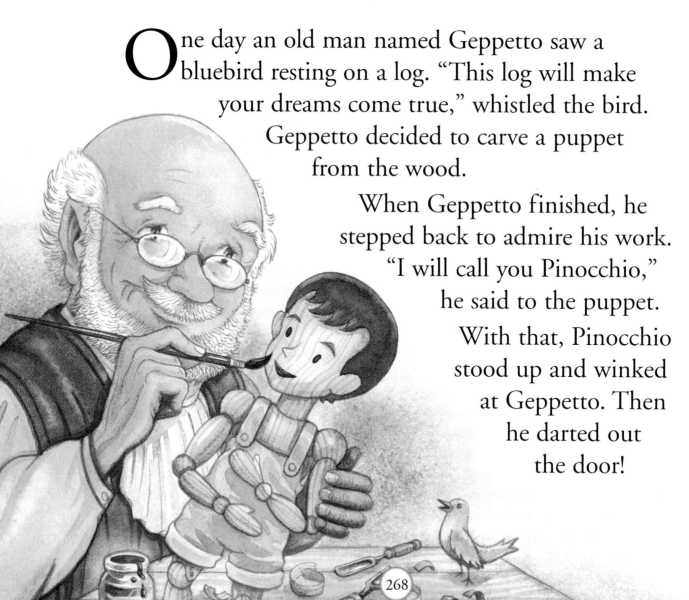

One day an old man named Geppetto saw a bluebird resting on a log. "This log will make your dreams come true," whistled the bird. Geppetto decided to carve a puppet from the wood.

When Geppetto finished, he stepped back to admire his work. "I will call you Pinocchio," he said to the puppet.

With that, Pinocchio stood up and winked at Geppetto. Then he darted out the door!

"Come back!" cried Geppetto.

But Pinocchio kept running. As he ran, his nose began to grow! From then on, whenever he was bad, Pinocchio's nose grew longer.

When a policeman saw the puppet, he grabbed him firmly by the nose. "You should be in school," he said.

"I'd rather play all day!" replied Pinocchio.

Out of breath, old Geppetto appeared and took Pinocchio back home.

Later that day, Geppetto gave Pinocchio two coins to buy a book for school. Pinocchio set off immediately. Soon he came upon two beggars who told Pinocchio that if he buried his money, it would grow into a money tree.

Just then, a bluebird called out, "Don't be foolish!"

But Pinocchio paid no attention.

The cat and fox showed Pinocchio where to bury his money, and told him to go away for a bit to allow the plant to grow.

When Pinocchio returned later, all
he found was an empty hole where he
had buried the coins. He had been tricked.

Overhead, Pinocchio heard the bird singing
again. He looked up to see a beautiful fairy.

"Pinocchio," she said, "if you are good, and if you
obey Geppetto, then one day you shall become a real
boy!" She swung Pinocchio onto her back and flew
him home.

"I promise to be good from now on," said a
hopeful Pinocchio.

On his way to school the next day, a man asked Pinocchio where he was going.

"To school," said Pinocchio.

"Why go to school when you can play?" asked the man. "Come with me to Playland."

Just then, a bluebird sang out, "Don't be foolish!" But Pinocchio paid no attention.

"Okay, I'll go," said Pinocchio.

And off they went.

Pinocchio

One day in Playland, something very surprising happened to Pinocchio. Because he had been bad for so long, he sprouted donkey ears— and a tail as well!

"I don't want to be a donkey. Hee-haw," cried Pinocchio.

Pinocchio heard a whistle and looked up to see the fairy. "I will take away your donkey ears and tail, but I cannot take you home," she said. "Your father is not there. He has been searching for you, and he is now lost at sea."

"I will search the sea until I find Geppetto!" said Pinocchio.

After several days of swimming, Pinocchio saw a giant whale. The whale yawned and swallowed Pinocchio! The scared puppet floated down into the whale's stomach.

"Is someone there?" said a quiet voice. A match flared, and Pinocchio saw Geppetto.

"Oh, Father, I have found you!" cried Pinocchio. The two embraced just as the whale's stomach shook violently.

Pinocchio

"The whale has the hiccups," said Geppetto. Suddenly, Pinocchio and Geppetto were hiccuped out of the whale. They swam back to the shore.

Pinocchio heard a familiar whistle and looked up to see the bluebird. "Brave Pinocchio," it sang, "all your misdeeds are forgiven. Be a good boy from now on."

At once Pinocchio felt different. "Look at me, Father!" he said. "I am a real live boy!"

The sight of his son brought tears of joy to Geppetto's eyes.

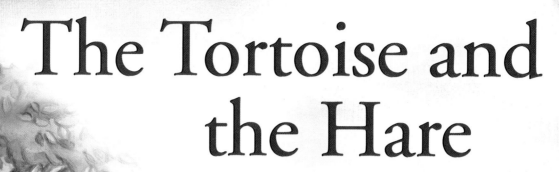

The Tortoise and the Hare

Adapted by David Presser

Illustrated by Viviana Diaz

In the woods there lived a very slow tortoise and a very swift hare. One bright morning, Tortoise was plodding along at his usual pace. Suddenly, Hare came bounding up to him.

"Good morning, Mr. Hare," said the friendly Tortoise. "My goodness, you are moving very quickly today."

"That I am, Tortoise!" said Hare. "But I cannot say the same for you."

"I am a very slow creature," Tortoise said, "but all the same, I would like to challenge you to a race."

"Oh Tortoise!" said Hare. "I could have run a race in the time it took you to make that challenge!"

Then Hare started to laugh so hard that he fell over. Other animals heard the noise. "What's the commotion?" they asked.

"This silly Tortoise has challenged me to a race!" said the Hare. "He is so slow that I won't even have to try hard to win."

The animals agreed on a course for the race, and Fox was chosen to act as the judge.

When it was time for the race to begin, Fox called out, "On your marks! Get set! Go!" Hare darted off, leaving Tortoise behind in a cloud of dust.

"Ha ha!" laughed Hare. "I'll show that old Tortoise! He should have known better than to think he could beat me." Soon, Hare was out of sight.

After a while, Hare thought "I am so far ahead of Tortoise that I think I'll rest here until he comes along. That will show him how foolish he is to race me!"

Hare stretched out on a very comfortable hammock and enjoyed a few tasty carrots. After he had eaten his fill, he felt sleepy. "Well, I suppose there is no harm in taking a little nap," Hare said to himself, and he soon fell fast asleep.

Meanwhile, Tortoise was happily moving along one step at a time, enjoying the scenery of the race course. After quite some time, he came upon the sleeping Hare. "Hello, friend Owl. Hello, friend Squirrel," Tortoise said quietly, so he would not wake Hare.

Tortoise continued on, enjoying the sun and the warm breeze.

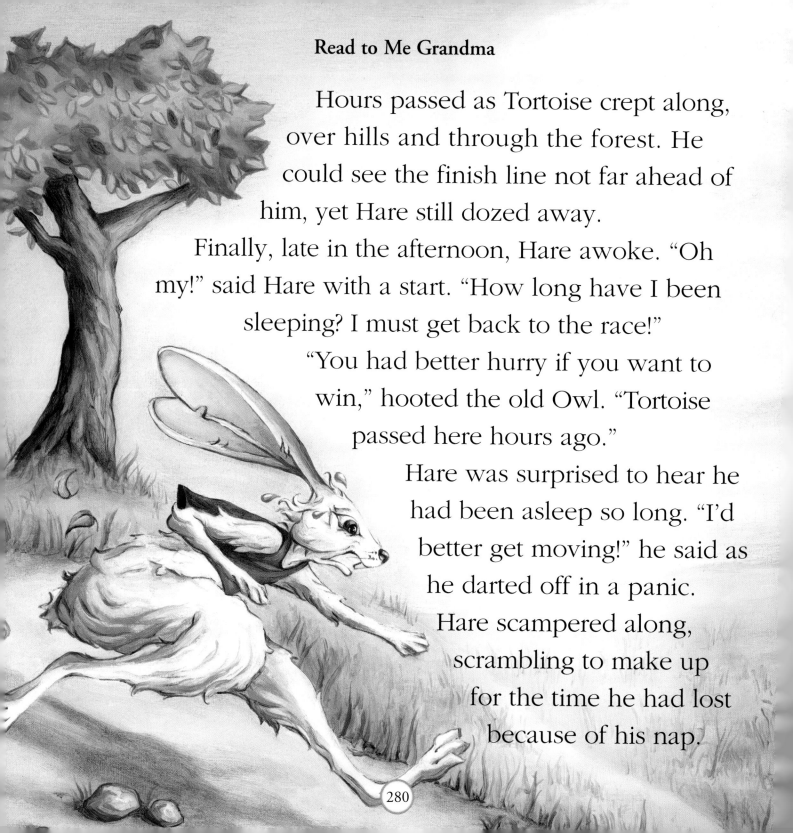

Hours passed as Tortoise crept along, over hills and through the forest. He could see the finish line not far ahead of him, yet Hare still dozed away.

Finally, late in the afternoon, Hare awoke. "Oh my!" said Hare with a start. "How long have I been sleeping? I must get back to the race!"

"You had better hurry if you want to win," hooted the old Owl. "Tortoise passed here hours ago."

Hare was surprised to hear he had been asleep so long. "I'd better get moving!" he said as he darted off in a panic. Hare scampered along, scrambling to make up for the time he had lost because of his nap.

Hare ran and ran. He went as fast as he could, but it was no use. When he ran over the last hill, he could see Tortoise ahead of him, crossing the finish line ever so slowly. "I declare Tortoise has beaten Hare!" shouted Fox.

As the animals cheered for Tortoise, Hare dragged himself to the finish line, out of breath. "How could you have beaten me?" said Hare. "You are so slow and I am so fast!"

"That is right, Mr. Hare," said Tortoise. "I may be slow, but I am steady, and I never stopped going. You see, slow and steady wins the race!"

281

Henny Penny

Adapted by Carolyn Quattrocki
Illustrated by Tim Ellis

One fine day Henny Penny was eating corn, when *boink*! An acorn suddenly fell off a tree and hit Henny Penny right on the top of her head.

"Oh my!" cried Henny Penny. "The sky is falling! I must go and tell the king!"

So Henny Penny tied a nice scarf around her head and set off down the road to tell the king that the sky was falling. On her way she passed the house of Cocky Locky, who was working hard to build a new porch. "Henny Penny, where are you going?" he asked.

"Cocky Locky, the sky is falling, and I am going to tell the king!" said Henny Penny.

"How do you know it is falling?" asked the friendly Cocky Locky.

"I saw it with my own eyes and heard it with my own ears," said Henny Penny. "And a piece of it fell on my head!"

"Then I will go with you to tell the king," said Cocky Locky. Henny Penny and Cocky Locky soon came across Ducky Lucky, who was enjoying a morning swim. "Good morning, Henny Penny and Cocky Locky," said Ducky Lucky. "Where are you going?"

"The sky is falling, and we are going to tell the king," said Cocky Locky.

"How do you know the sky is falling?" asked Ducky Lucky.

"Henny Penny told me," said Cocky Locky.

283

"I saw it with my own eyes and heard it with my own ears," said Henny Penny. "And a piece of it fell on my head!"

"Then I will go with both of you to tell the king," said Ducky Lucky.

Henny Penny, Cocky Locky, and Ducky Lucky went along until they met Goosey Loosey at the market. "Good morning, Henny Penny, Cocky Locky, and Ducky Lucky," said Goosey Loosey. "Where are you going?"

"The sky is falling, and we are going to tell the king," said Ducky Lucky.

"How do you know the sky is falling?" asked Goosey Loosey.

"Cocky Locky told me," said Ducky Lucky.

"Henny Penny told me," said Cocky Locky.

"I saw it with my own eyes and heard it with my own ears," said Henny Penny. "And a piece of it fell on my head!"

"Then I will go with all of you to tell the king," said Goosey Loosey.

Henny Penny, Cocky Locky, Ducky Lucky, and Goosey Loosey all went along until they met Turkey Lurkey as she was walking through her garden gate.

"Good morning, Henny Penny, Cocky Locky, Ducky Lucky, and Goosey Loosey," said Turkey Lurkey. "Where are you going?"

"The sky is falling, and we are going to tell the king," said Goosey Loosey.

"How do you know the sky is falling?" asked Turkey Lurkey.

"Ducky Lucky told me," said Goosey Loosey.

"Cocky Locky told me," said Ducky Lucky.

"Henny Penny told me," said Cocky Locky.

"I saw it with my own eyes and heard it with my own ears," said Henny Penny. "And a piece of it fell on my head!"

"Then I will go with all of you to tell the king," said Turkey Lurkey.

They all went along until they met Foxy Loxy. "Good morning," said Foxy Loxy. "Where are you going?"

"The sky is falling, and we are going to tell the king," said Turkey Lurkey.

"How do you know the sky is falling?" asked the clever Foxy Loxy.

"Goosey Loosey told me," said Turkey Lurkey.

"Ducky Lucky told me," said Goosey Loosey.

"Cocky Locky told me," said Ducky Lucky.

"Henny Penny told me," said Cocky Locky.

"I saw it with my own eyes and heard it with my own ears," said Henny Penny. "And a piece of it fell on my head!"

"Then come with me," said Foxy Loxy. "I will show you a shorter way to the king's palace."

They all followed Foxy Loxy, and soon they came to the entrance of a dark cave. What they did not know was that this dark cave was really Foxy Loxy's home!

"Just follow me through here," said Foxy Loxy, "and we will soon be at the king's palace."

Henny Penny, Cocky Locky, Ducky Lucky, Goosey Loosey, and Turkey Lurkey all followed Foxy Loxy into the cave. Henny Penny was last in line, and she was frightened. She started to run away.

Henny Penny ran and ran as fast as her legs would carry her. She ran back along the long road. She ran across the narrow bridge. And she ran down the steep hill.

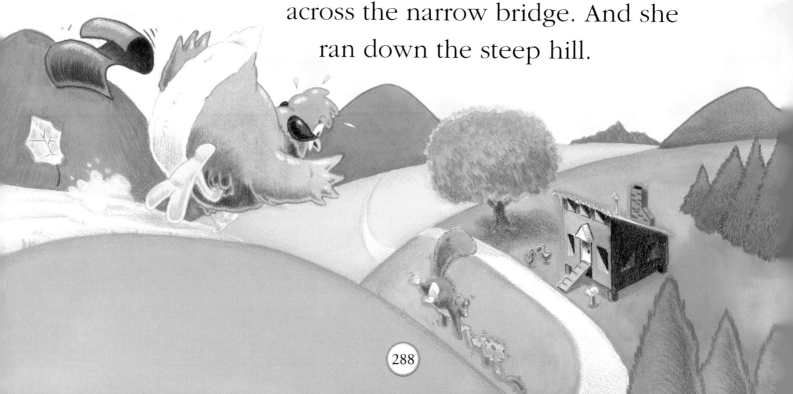

Henny Penny

Henny Penny quickly ran past Turkey Lurkey's garden. She ran past the market where Goosey Loosey had been buying some food. She ran past Ducky Lucky's pond, and she ran past Cocky Locky's house.

Henny Penny ran and ran until, up ahead, she saw her cozy little house with the oak tree beside it. She could even see the corn scattered on the ground underneath the tree.

Henny Penny ran all the way home! She was last seen scratching happily for corn in her little yard.

And the king never did hear from Henny Penny or anyone else that the sky was falling.

Beauty and the Beast

From the adaptation by Amy Adair
Illustrated by David Merrell

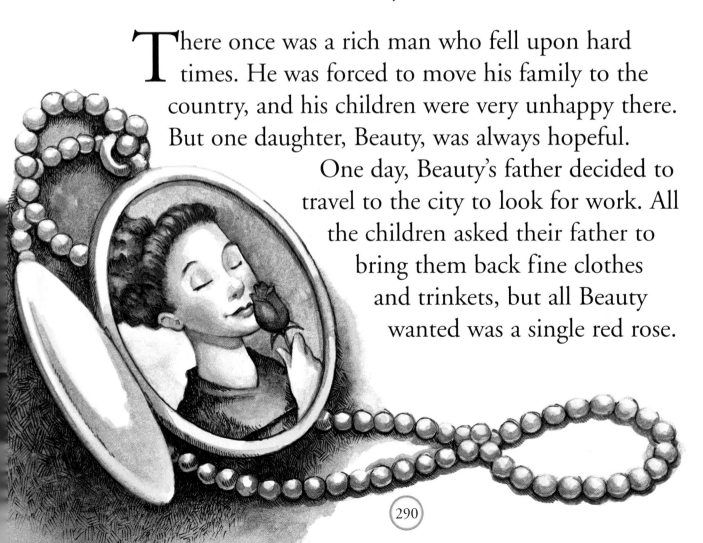

There once was a rich man who fell upon hard times. He was forced to move his family to the country, and his children were very unhappy there. But one daughter, Beauty, was always hopeful.

One day, Beauty's father decided to travel to the city to look for work. All the children asked their father to bring them back fine clothes and trinkets, but all Beauty wanted was a single red rose.

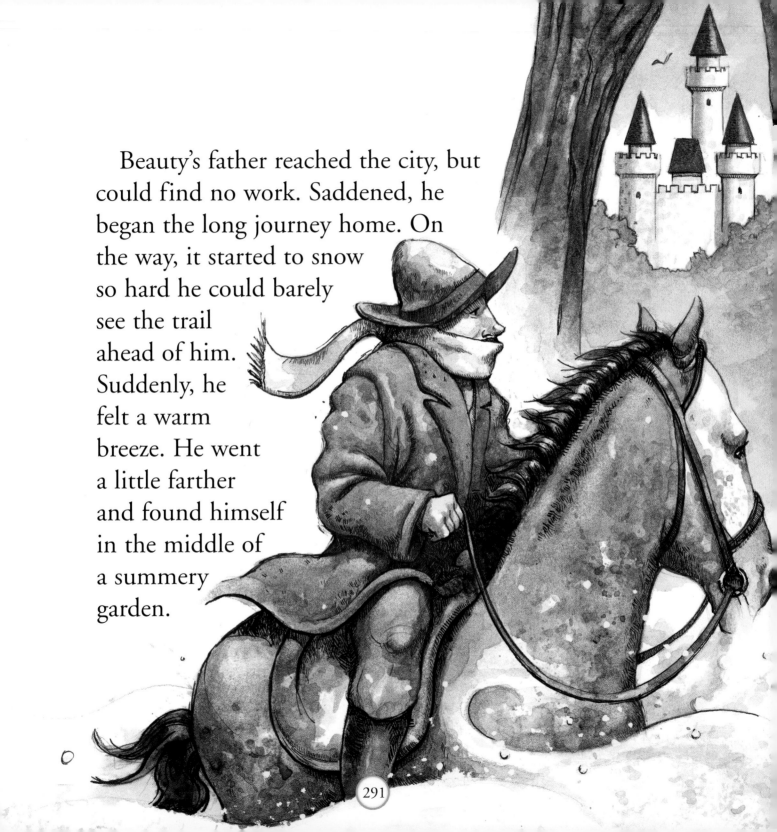

Beauty's father reached the city, but could find no work. Saddened, he began the long journey home. On the way, it started to snow so hard he could barely see the trail ahead of him. Suddenly, he felt a warm breeze. He went a little farther and found himself in the middle of a summery garden.

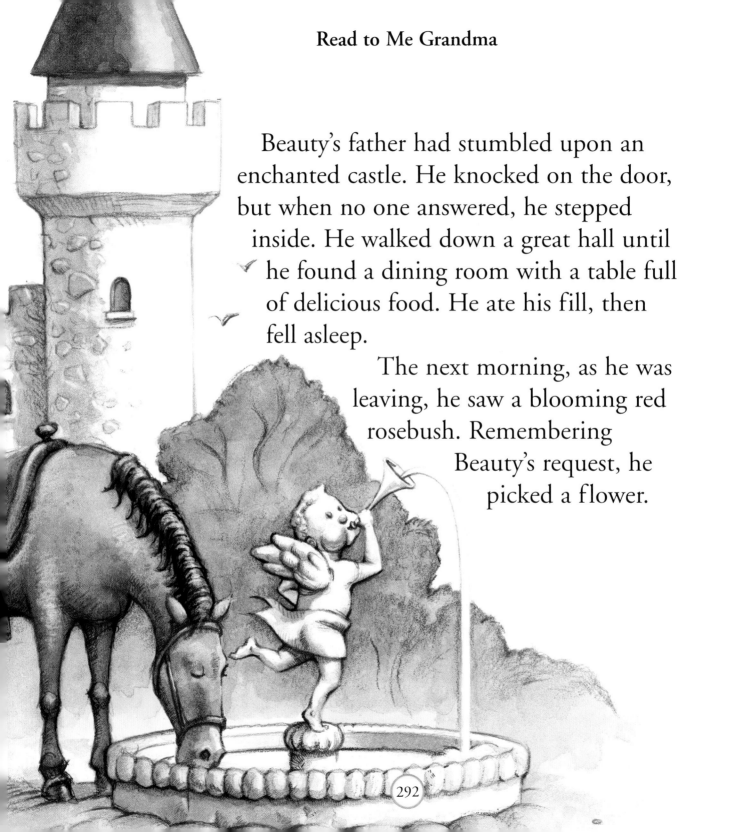

Beauty's father had stumbled upon an enchanted castle. He knocked on the door, but when no one answered, he stepped inside. He walked down a great hall until he found a dining room with a table full of delicious food. He ate his fill, then fell asleep.

The next morning, as he was leaving, he saw a blooming red rosebush. Remembering Beauty's request, he picked a flower.

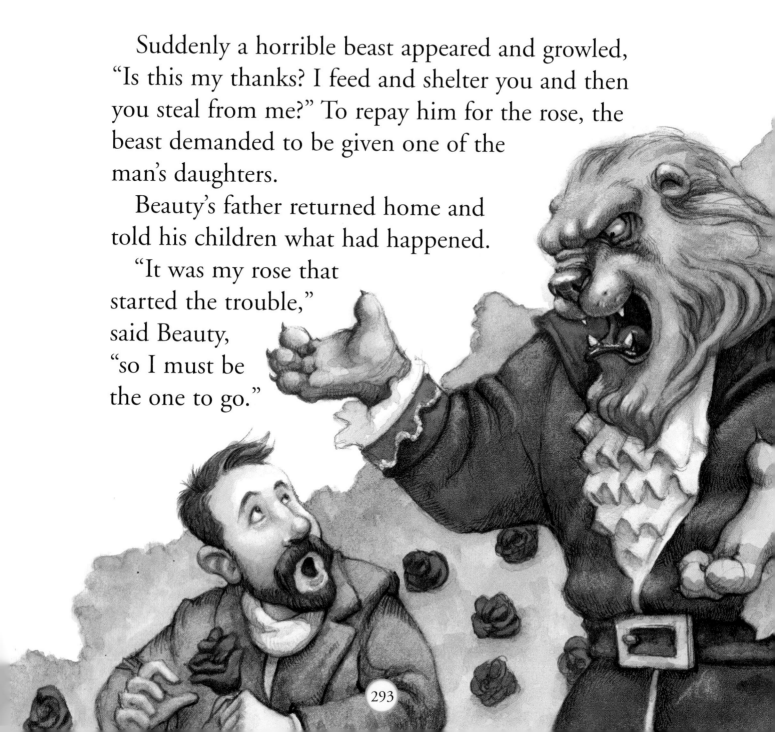

Suddenly a horrible beast appeared and growled, "Is this my thanks? I feed and shelter you and then you steal from me?" To repay him for the rose, the beast demanded to be given one of the man's daughters.

Beauty's father returned home and told his children what had happened.

"It was my rose that started the trouble," said Beauty, "so I must be the one to go."

The next day, Beauty
arrived at the beast's castle. She saw that the
beast's eyes were kind, and she was not afraid.

Beauty quickly made the castle her home. Every
night she dined with the gentle beast. Beauty grew to
be quite fond of him.

One night, Beauty asked the beast if she could go
home for a visit. The beast agreed that she could go
home for two months.

The beast gave Beauty a trunk full of gifts to take to her family. He also gave her a magic ring with a large red jewel. The ring would take her home when she turned it on her finger.

When Beauty magically appeared at home, her family was thrilled to see her. She gave them the trunk full of gifts, and they all marveled at the beast's generosity.

Beauty enjoyed being with her family, but soon she began to miss the beast.

One night, Beauty looked deep into the jewel and saw the beast lying in his garden. He seemed to be dying! Distraught, she turned the ring on her finger and magically returned to the castle.

Beauty rushed to the beast's side. "Oh, please do not die!" she cried. "I never knew it before, but I love you!"

"Will you marry me, Beauty?" the beast whispered. "Yes," Beauty answered breathlessly.

Suddenly there was a flash of light, and the beast changed into a handsome prince!

"An enchantress put me under an evil spell—only true love could free me," the prince explained. "Your love broke the spell!"

The prince sent for Beauty's family, and he and Beauty were married the next day. They all lived happily ever after in the enchanted castle.

The Elves and the Shoemaker

From the adaptation by Jennifer Boudart
Illustrated by Kristen Goeters

One harsh winter, a poor shoemaker and his wife discovered that they had only enough leather left to make one pair of shoes. After the leather was gone, they would have no way to make a living, for they could not afford any more.

"Things will work out," said the shoemaker. He cut out the leather and went to bed, planning to finish the shoes the next day.

In the morning, instead of the pieces of leather, the shoemaker found a marvelous pair of shoes! The shoes were beautifully made, with fantastic detail. *Who could have made these?* he wondered, amazed.

That day, a rich tourist came into the shoemaker's shop. "I've stepped in a puddle of sludge, and I simply can't walk around in these muddy shoes," he said. "Do you have anything in my size?"

The shoemaker and his wife showed him the mysterious shoes. They were a perfect fit! "These are the loveliest shoes I've ever seen!" exclaimed the traveler, giving the shoemaker a shiny gold coin to pay for them.

With the gold coin, the shoemaker bought enough leather to make two pairs of shoes. Once again the shoemaker cut the leather and placed the pieces on his workbench. The next morning he found two more pairs of fabulous finished shoes.

This continued for many nights, until the shoemaker's shelves were filled with beautiful shoes like no one had ever seen before.

Word of the shoemaker's fine shoes soon made him the most popular shoemaker in the land. But still something bothered him. One evening he said to his wife, "Every night, someone works hard to help us. It's a shame we don't even know who it is. Why don't we stay up to find out?"

That night, just like always, the shoemaker cut leather into pieces and placed them on his workbench. But instead of going to bed, he and his wife hid in the doorway.

Soon two elves appeared on the workbench! Their clothes were old and ragged, and they must have been quite cold. Nevertheless, they worked happily all through the night.

"Clearly they are in great need," said the shoemaker, "yet they work all night to help us."

The shoemaker's wife had an idea. "Let's make those little elves the clothes they need!" she said. That evening, instead of leaving leather on the bench, they left tiny new clothes and shoes.

The elves magically appeared at midnight. They climbed upon the workbench and saw the two tiny suits. Their little faces brightened and they shouted gleefully. At once they put on the fine new suits and shoes. They were so excited they began to dance and sing.

After that night, the elves never came back. But the shoemaker and his wife did not mind. They were just glad they had been able to help. The shoemaker remained successful for the rest of his days, and he and his wife never forgot the kindness of the two little strangers.

The Three Little Pigs

Adapted by Jennifer Boudart
Illustrated by Judith Mitchell

It was a fine day in the forest. The sun shone brightly through the trees, and its warmth cheered three little pigs who had just left the home they grew up in. The pigs were brothers who hoped to find a new home of their own. A grassy meadow in the middle of the forest seemed to be the perfect spot.

"What a wonderful place to make a new start," said the oldest brother proudly.

"Now that we have found a good spot," said the youngest brother, "let's have lunch." So the little pigs spread out a blanket and ate their lunch while making some plans.

The brothers agreed they should build a house right away. Each brother had a different idea about what kind of house to build. The youngest brother, who was also the laziest, suggested a straw house. The middle brother, who had a bit more sense, thought using wood was a better idea. But the oldest brother made the most sense. "Though it is true, wood is certainly good, bricks are simply the best," he said.

The brothers could not agree. In the end, they decided to build three houses. The youngest brother built his house out of straw, and the middle brother built his out of wood. The oldest brother was the last to finish. While his brothers took naps in the sun, he worked and worked until his brick house was complete, chimney and all.

The brothers had a picnic to celebrate. Proudly, they stood back and admired their three homes.

The three little pigs soon had visitors from all around the forest. One bright morning, the youngest pig heard a knock on his door. Who could it be?

"Let me in," growled a deep voice.

The young pig peeked through a space in the straw wall. A huge, hairy wolf crouched outside his door. He had large teeth, and he looked hungry!

"Not by the hair on my chinny chin chin!" said the young pig.

The wolf snarled. He was very, very hungry.

The Three Little Pigs

"Then I'll huff, and I'll puff, and I'll blow your house down!" roared the wolf.

The wolf let out a blast of air. S-W-O-O-O-S-H! The straw went flying! Then the wolf spotted the little pig pushing himself through the window of the wooden house next door.

The wolf ran to the door of the wooden house. "Let me in!" snapped the angry wolf. Inside the house, the two brothers hugged each other in fear.

"Not by the hair on our chinny chin chins!" they yelled.

"Then I'll huff, and I'll puff, and I'll blow your house down!" roared the big, bad wolf.

Once again, the wolf blew with all of his might. C-R-R-R-A-C-K! All of the boards snapped like twigs.

The little pigs ran to the brick house next door and squeezed down the chimney. The two homeless pigs told their brother about the wolf and their ruined houses. Outside, the wolf licked his lips as he knocked on the door. “Let me in!” he hollered in his meanest, wolfiest voice.

“Not by the hair on our chinny chin chins,” said the oldest pig, quietly and calmly.

“Then I’ll huff, and I’ll puff, and I’ll blow your house down!” cried the wolf. He blew his biggest breath yet, but the house was still standing! The wolf blew again. Not a single brick budged!

The pigs heard the wolf jump on the roof. Quickly, the oldest brother lit a fire in the fireplace. Then he sat down to warm his hands.

With a giant crash, the wolf fell down the chimney and landed in the flames. "Let me out!" howled the wolf as he ran in circles. And that's just what the three little pigs did. The wolf ran off and never bothered any of them again.

The three brothers still live in the middle of the forest. They still have picnics and take turns visiting each other's homes. But all of their houses are now made of brick.

Rapunzel

From the adaptation by Jennifer Boudart
Illustrated by Kathi Ember

A poor couple lived next door to a witch who had a lush garden.
One evening the wife, who was going to have a baby, said to her husband, "I would love to eat some of the witch's sweet Rapunzel lettuce."

The caring husband crept into the witch's garden. As he picked a head of lettuce, it began to scream!

The witch appeared and said, "Take all the lettuce you want. But in return, you must give me your baby when it is born."

Terrified, the man ran home. He did not tell his wife what the witch had said. Surely he could think of a way to break the promise.

The next morning, the wife had a baby girl and named her Rapunzel. The witch came and took the baby that very day.

The witch took Rapunzel to live in a tower in the middle of nowhere. The witch was kind to Rapunzel, and loved her like a daughter. But she would not let Rapunzel leave the tower.

The years passed, and Rapunzel grew to be a lovely young woman with long, shiny golden hair. But she was very lonely. She had never even seen another person besides the witch.

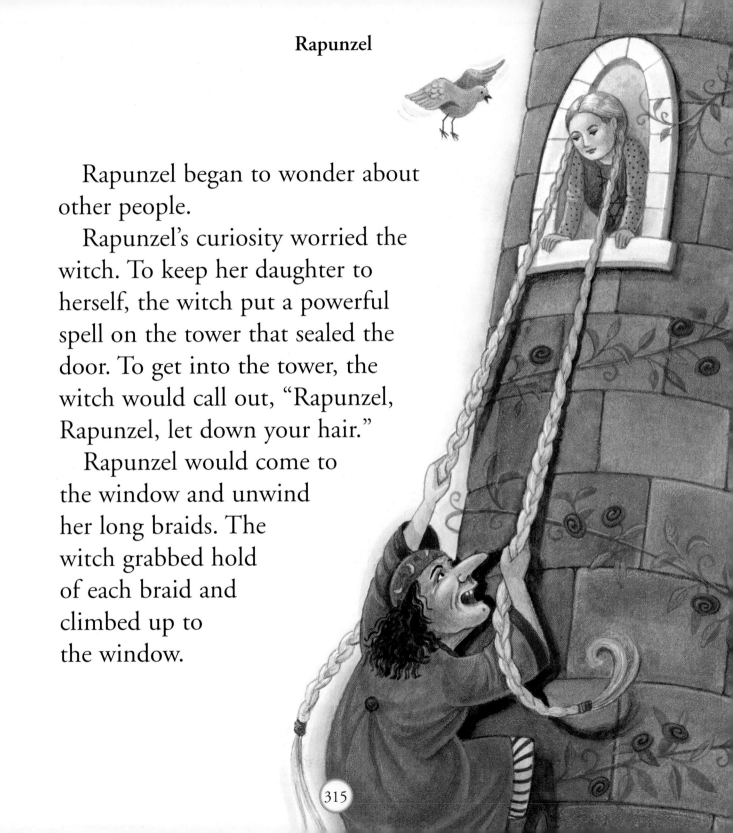

Rapunzel

Rapunzel began to wonder about other people.

Rapunzel's curiosity worried the witch. To keep her daughter to herself, the witch put a powerful spell on the tower that sealed the door. To get into the tower, the witch would call out, "Rapunzel, Rapunzel, let down your hair."

Rapunzel would come to the window and unwind her long braids. The witch grabbed hold of each braid and climbed up to the window.

One morning, a prince was exploring his kingdom when he saw an isolated tower in the distance. Through his telescope, he watched an old woman walk up to the tower and shout, "Rapunzel, Rapunzel, let down your hair."

A beautiful maiden appeared and hung her braids out the window. The old woman used them to climb the tower wall.

Rapunzel

Before long, the maiden dropped her braids again, and the old woman climbed back down and disappeared into the woods.

The prince approached the tower. He tried to open the door, but it was sealed tightly shut.

"Rapunzel, Rapunzel, let down your hair," he called.

The maiden unwrapped her hair, and the prince climbed inside the tower.

"Who are you?" he asked.

Rapunzel told the prince her story.

"I can take you away from this tower," said the prince, "and you can be free."

Rapunzel knew this could be her only chance to escape. She let down her hair so the prince could climb down. Then Rapunzel closed her eyes and jumped, landing safely in the prince's arms.

As they rode away, Rapunzel and the prince talked and talked.

Rapunzel was delighted to speak to someone other than the witch. When they came to a little village, they passed a shack where an old man and woman were working in their garden. When they overheard the prince call the girl Rapunzel, they looked at each other. Instantly, they knew that this must be their long-lost daughter, and they called out to the prince to stop.

And so, after many years, the family was finally reunited. They lived in happiness together forever after.

The End